LURED

TRIBES, #3

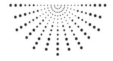

MILANA JACKS

PROLOGUE

TRIBES SERIES QUICK REFERENCE

Tribes series takes place on a planet called Nomra Prime. Thus far, we have the Ka and the Ra tribe that signed a peace treaty after eons of wars. On both sides, females and young are almost nonexistent, and the Ka males are near extinction.

Their alien classification is *Predator*. They're dual-form aliens. Their hunting form is a hunter and often stands as tall as a horse with exposed large sharp teeth, meaning the hunter's lips don't cover the teeth. They have large erect ears, which make them appear bigger and more frightening. They're extremely fit and agile, and can execute leaps we (humans) consider impossible.

Most tribes can be united under a single "King" they designate by adding -i to the tribe name. So for Ka tribe, it's Kai where -i at the end indicates a male who is a leader of the Ka tribe, the top of their food chain and this male always eats first.

Inside a single tribe, an earl governs a smaller territory called an earldom. There can be many many earldoms in any one tribe.

Portal: a spatial shortcut to another place on the planet. A closed portal, meaning a vertical golden line, is not visible to the human eye.

Main Characters:

Hart : Ka tribal leader, Alpha of the Ka tribe. His designation is Kai.

Stephanie: Hart's human. Believed to be Amti.

Nar: Hart's brother and second strongest of the Ka males.

Michelle: Nar's human.

Mas: Ka tribe portal genius.

Tis: Mas's brother.

Ark: Ra tribe's Alpha, meaning the strongest of the Ra males but not an elected leader, meaning the Ra do not have a single "King" named Rai where -i at the end indicates his "kingship" over other tribal members. Hart's frenemy.

Sha-male: a male who performs religious rites, sacrifices, prayers (priest, imam, etc)

Gur: Earl in the Ra tribe. Wants war.

Feli: Second to Gur in Gur's earldom.

The Lore: Tribes worship the female. Goddesses are admired, feared, and respected. Goddess are believed to be returning as human females so that they may walk the lands again.

Bera: Goddess of fertility and war.

Aimea: Goddess of doom. Most feared.

Herea: Goddess of hunt and harmony. Most popular.

Amti: Goddess of madness and lust.

Aoa: Goddess of thunder and pain. Patron goddess of the Ka tribe.

Eme: Goddess of blood and grace. Also called the Blood-letter. Herea's daughter.

Mae: Goddess of fire and lies. Aoa's mother.

Locations:

Kalia: Ka tribe capital. Near the Ra border. Suffered extensive structural damage during the wars.

Blood Dunes: Ancient grounds haunted by Eme, the Bloodletter. Currently, Ra territory under governance of earl Tash, Ark's brother.

TBA as the series rolls ...

CHAPTER ONE

MAS

In the middle of the night, instead of sleeping and healing, bleary-eyed and mighty annoyed with my state of mind, I stare at my private portal controls. I hacked the portal control center Feli erected during the Ra games. All I have to do now is pull up the portal he shoved me into and step onto the sand just beyond the shimmering opening. I even packed my sack, strapped on weapons, and brought a gift I made during the cycle when I couldn't stop thinking about the footprint with five small toes.

The fact I wanna find a female isn't unusual.

The fact I wanna go off to look for the female near the Blood Dunes is unusual.

It's unlike me to risk my life when I know I can't win. And when faced with a female who could be a goddess, a male cannot win. They have a way of crawling under the skin and wrapping their claws around our hunters' necks, stroking those instincts for both breeding and hunting, making us more predatory than we want to be, making us obsess over them and serve them till the end of our time.

Standing, I rub the back of my neck. If I tell Hart where

I'm going, he'll prohibit it. Or worse, send me in with a group of Ka males, risking their lives as well as mine in the process. We're just over one thousand males, and every male counts, or we'll be wiped from the face of the planet, become a historical swirl on a wall commemorating the Ra conquests.

Before I can talk myself out of this, I jump into the portal and land on the sand of the Blood Dunes. I don't linger. The moment my boots touch the sand, I sprint for the thick forests surrounding the Dunes on three sides.

My tracks. Crap. I walk back and scratch out my tracks with the ax and keep covering them, running backward, bent over and all kinds of awkward and slow. But I don't want the womankind (or goddess) to know I arrived. I need to catch her unawares, and I need an exit portal inside the forest for that to happen. I am not going back on the damned sand where my ancestors lay bleeding for span after span, unable to heal, unable to die, while the goddess of blood and grace danced, hopping from body to body, evoking her favorite song made by the wheezing of their lungs beneath her perfect foot. With five small toes.

Leaping now, because I can't get the fuck out of there fast enough, I land on the rock and hop to another, then another, until I reach the upper part of the rock-strewn forest. Having safely made it past the sand, I settle between two boulders and get out the ritual stones and the wood. On the ground, I arrange them into the pattern that will signal a sacrifice to the goddess of blood and grace and then cut my palm with a knife, wincing at the pain. She's fond of bleeding predators.

I clench my fist so my blood drips over the wood and stones, then light a fire and snuff it out before the fire goddess, Mae, decides it's for her. Smoke rises, and I wave my hand to direct it toward me and inhale the body of Eme, goddess of blood and grace. *There ya go, female. Mas loves you.*

6

Fuck off now, and let me have the human sans your bloodthirsty spirit.

I glance at the cut on my hand. It's not healing as quickly as usual. I stare at it, willing it to close up. Nothing. Good, this is good. It means I've done the ritual as the Sha-male instructed and not fucked it up. I'll recover soon.

Something zips past above me, and I duck. When I hear the whistle of it farther away, I lift my head.

A round white pod, much like the two pods I've secured on our main tower over in Kalia, lands on the sand. I perk up, anticipating my first view of the human female and inwardly congratulate myself on finding her. Who needs Ark to deliver females when they have Mas the portal master, hm? Gonna tell my Kai that when I bring this one in.

Oh yes. I rub my palms and wince. The bloody palm isn't healing, and I can't stand it. Apprehension that I might be in the presence of divinity makes me itchy. I scratch my back on the rock behind me.

The pod door pops open, and the first thing I see is a pointed foot with five toes. I suppress a joyful squeal. I'll squeal plenty with my tribemates as I set up the portal controls for our games. I'm not even telling them which goddess I think she is or where I got her from. Nobody would compete for the daughter of Herea. I really ought to hand her over to the Ra, let them drink their blood while they wail like terriks during the mating cycle.

A leg extends, and her toes touch the sand. A long, finely shaped leg. Real long. Almost as long as mine, but thinner, prettier, feminine. The other leg joins the first, and then I see hands running up and down the leg, spreading glistening oil over the skin. The movement of her arms, also long and thin, and graceful hands entraps me, and briefly, I imagine those slender hands stroking my abdomen and lower yet.

I fix my erection, shift a little, and crouch, leaning my

elbow on the rock that I should be using to hide my position, not as a place for ogling a female who might bleed me for a turn or more if she doesn't have anything else to do. And there's nothing to do out here.

She steps out of the pod and inhales deeply, closes her eyes for a moment. Her golden hair is pulled tightly in a high neat bun, and her face is…well, one of a goddess, meant to be admired and worshiped and lusted over. She's tall, and she's rubbing some kind of oil over her nude body. Although thin, she's strong and curvy at the same time. In fact, her fitness is quite uncanny and unexpected.

And soon I find out why.

The womankind walks away from the pod with her toes pointing forward, then rises on said toes and starts dancing, extending and bending one long leg at the knee while twirling in a fast cycle that makes my head spin. If I had any doubt that the goddess of grace walks the Blood Dunes again, I don't anymore. I'm glued to my position, unable to take my eyes off her or move to snatch her while she's distracted in her dance, leaping from one leg to another, executing splits nobody in our lands can replicate. It's not only the legs. The way her entire body moves gives an impression of a feather swaying on the wind. It's…it's mesmerizing, and I purr as I rise a little more so I can admire her dance.

The breeze picks up her scent and sends it to me. I inhale a lungful, and my balls are so happy, they almost jingle together. She's the most graceful of…prey. I lick my teeth, my gums swelling. Fuck, I'm hungry and horny, and her flesh would satisfy both needs. I knock on my head to be sure I'm not winded. Still something ringing in there, so that's good.

I continue watching from afar. She's so beautiful when she's unaware that anyone is watching. Most prey are, but none provide admirable entertainment like this one.

Hart said womankind don't leap.

He said they're awkwardly uncoordinated.

That's because he's never seen Eme dance. But he will as soon as I bring her in. All there's left for me to do is find her nesting place, open a portal into Kalia, and let her walk through. This is gonna be so easy.

Mm-hm.

CHAPTER TWO

TATYANA

If you had to live on a deserted island for a month, what three things would you bring with you? Yeah, I've seen the question on social media multiple times. Several times, I even answered it, usually with something like *a good book, a violin, and a pair of pointe shoes*. Now, after I've crashed on a deserted beach on Joylius and spent a few weeks or maybe a month here, awaiting National Security (or anyone, really) to pick up my pod's signal and rescue me, my answers change daily. Some days, I need a sharp dagger, sunscreen, and a tent with a bed. Other days, I need directions to mainland Joylius, prepped and ready-to-eat meat, and some dick to take the edge off.

When stranded in a place of landing that has shelter, food, and fresh water, one doesn't leave until exhausting all other options first. I haven't exhausted anything yet, though I can't exist here for a year either. I might go crazy all alone. Besides, I hate bleeding animals for survival. The guilt's making me starve, and that's not good since I'm anemic and could collapse at any time.

· · ·

When I first crashed, I waited on the beach, expecting more pods to land in the same place, but so far, I haven't seen a soul. Not Joylius natives or humans, and not even one of the warrior species that patrol Joylius.

I'm pretty sure they'll find me. Eventually.

I've signaled plenty and keep the pod running daily so they can pick up my signal. Someone will find me out here, preferably before I run out of shits to give and go insane without any contact. I haven't spoken in over a month, not even to myself, though the second I do, I might as well declare insanity. My mom talked to herself all the time. She also stabbed herself with scissors trying to dig out her liver.

I collapse on the ground for a few minutes to catch my breath. Who knew dancing barefoot in the sand would feel so rewarding? I practically lived in my shoes, and seeing as Denver doesn't have a beach, I never practiced on sand. When I get back, maybe I will. Maybe I'll finally leave Denver and the memories of Mom and my ex behind. Maybe this experience will somehow profoundly change me. Maybe I'll summon the guts to quit accepting new gigs.

Forty-one is a nice retirement age for me, and I'm at the peak of my career, so I would exit voluntarily and with grace. Maybe I'll take Harold's offer and teach. Maybe I'll retire on Joylius and shag a sexy man half my age who takes me rough and hard at night and serves me margaritas during the day. Maybe I can even think about having a child. The possibilities are endless.

I giggle and shield my eyes from the sun. Dreaming keeps me alive, I swear it.

Crawling on the sand, I make it to the water. It's fresh water, not salty, so I drink some before diving in and cooling off from my morning routine. There're some flowers that grow on the trees around here that ooze oils and pleasant scents I've used to rub into my hair and body so at least I'm not stinky all day.

I dive under the clear water, and a school of colorful fish rushes me. I squint and bat at them with my hands because they're practically attacking me by the millions, tickling me all over. Once they pass, I continue swimming deeper into the sea.

Something massive, horned, and scaled with one eye the size of a football is gunning for me. It's a one-eyed horned anaconda. Jesus! I surface and freestyle toward the coast as fast as my arms and legs can move.

The sea creature rises from behind me, casting a massive shadow on the beach, and I freeze. The fear of knowing I'm gonna die before anyone can find me grips me and cramps all my muscles. The creature screeches, and I cover my ears at the same time that the waves throws me onto the beach. This seems to make me able to move again, and I scramble up, then sprint away from the water.

Bending, trying to catch my breath, I turn. The creature's tail whips over the water as it struggles to overpower a land animal that's lodged its teeth into the sea creature's throat. The land animal snaps its jaws at the massive horned anaconda's neck. Blood gushes as if someone turned on a fountain, spraying all over the water and sand, droplets hitting my toes. I wiggle them, then look back at the scene.

The land animal, ten times smaller than the creature, is a vicious-looking horse from hell. He (or she, but I'm going with he) holds the side of the creature's neck between his teeth and kind of just stands there in the shallow sea.

An eerie calm settles in the air as he watches me with orange eyes and black, vertically slit pupils. He's got a massive head and huge ears.

Slowly, I backpedal toward my pod and make it inside. Closing the door, I watch through the pod's screen as the hell horse swims toward the rocks. Carrying the anaconda seems hard for him, and he stumbles over the lower rocks he's jumping on. His feet are bent backward, almost like a frog's and they pad carefully across the rocks, almost like a feline readying to leap. He rears back, weight completely on his back legs, and springs up, executing a...seventy-foot leap and landing on a large flat rock. The animal turns and drops the anaconda, keeping his head down, ears low, eyes on my pod.

I zoom in on him on the screen.

He's got giant sharp teeth, fish flesh stuck between them that he cleans off with a single swipe of his tongue. Settling on his belly, he rips into the creature and eats, eyes never leaving my pod, as if I intend to steal his meal. No fucking way. Fish is a great source of iron, but I'd like to live longer if I can. I don't even touch my cousin's Yorkie while he eats for fear he'll nip my fingers.

I fire up the pod and return to the clearing in the forest I've called home since I crashed. I park the pod in the place I've flagged with strips of red cloth tied to sticks. The pod shakes as I try to maneuver it, and I stick my tongue between my lips as I concentrate on not crash-landing.

On Earth, I've never piloted an airborne vehicle, but let me tell ya, this experience has taught me all kinds of things, and not just about flying.

I can start a fire.

I can extract oil from plants.

I can even hunt.

The pod lands with a thump, and I cringe, wishing these stupid things had legs I could unfold and land on. They don't. It's just a round thing with a small flattened area at the bottom. These pods aren't meant for piloting at all. They belong on spaceships, and in case of emergency, they're enough to fly toward the destination or the nearest space station where they can dock. Or so the preflight briefing told us. Nobody ever listens to those preflight speeches. Yeah, well, they should. When I get back to Earth, maybe I'll video a memoir about this experience.

The pod shuts off, but I stay inside for a while and scan the clearing for signs of animals like the one who, technically, saved my life. None found, I pop open the exit. It gets stuck again. I shoulder it open, grunting. The door grinds as it opens, and I wince at the loud disruption in the normally quiet forest. Sand got in the track. Another thing I'll have to figure out how to clean.

The reason I picked this place to camp is the already-set-up fireplace with seven logs. It seems to me like someone had camped here. Probably one of the warrior species we're in alliance with rested here while patrolling Joylius. I found two spears and even a nice sharp knife nearby. I also found a pelt. Bloody but beggars can't be choosers. Nights here are brutal and the pelt keeps me warm.

Sitting on the log, I grab the large leaf I collect fresh water in and drink, then eat some fruit I found growing on trees, wondering if the hell horse would attack me. Most animals leave humans alone. Or so I've heard. Still, I'll keep the knife nearby today.

CHAPTER THREE

MAS

Yelon, a rarely spotted viperfish that lives in deep seas, is a once-in-a-lifetime meal that I savor and lick and toss around playfully, rejoicing in the taste. The nice large juicy meal will last me for several spans. Rich in minerals, it also makes the transition from male to hunter easier because the minerals it contains lubricates my joints and pumps the muscles full of strength at the same time.

I'm buzzing with energy, mainly aggression, and itching for a fight. Or a fuck. A fuck would be good. Haven't ever fucked. Most of us haven't. Except for Hart and Nar, which makes me wanna kick them in the balls.

Standing, I turn up my ass, wiggle it as I stretch, first the front, then the hind legs, then my spine. I burp, then hack up a large piece of yelon. Oh, a cheekbone. I eat it back up, this time crunching it well. Yummy.

There's still more than half the fish left, and I look around, growling as if someone's gonna appear out of thin air and take my food. If I leave it here, even for a few spans, it'll still be fine.

But I can't leave my food.

Is the female hungry?

If I dropped it off wherever she's staying, would she eat yelon? Of course she would. Womankind have no qualms about eating the flesh of their predators. We eat only our prey. We do not consume the flesh of other predators, meaning we do not consume Ra hunters. Or any other species that we recognize as equals.

I shudder at the thought of eating another hunter, and my meal threatens to spill. Better stop thinking about Amti, Hart's human, eating Sor.

I take the thickest part of the viperfish between my teeth and prepare for climbing. Sitting back on my hind legs, I tap around the rock's surface, searching for a rough, nonslippery part so I can execute a difficult climb, especially now that I'm carrying both my sack and my food.

I bounce and land almost at the top of my destination, claws scraping the rock, my grip slipping. I drop the prey and claw my way up, then turn around and look down to where my food dropped between two rocks. No hunter dies for its prey. Instinct made me either drop the food or slip down. In hunter, decision-making takes no time.

Leaving the prey, I move toward the dense forest where I saw the womankind taking the pod, then hovering it above a specific place, which I presume is her camp. In the forest, small animals quiet down. A big green bug zips past my nose. Oh, a snack. I pause and wait for another. *Bzzzz.* I snap it up and crunch on it as I move along. Bug guts spill onto my tongue, and I lick my teeth. I love sweet liquid on my tongue.

The steep mountain takes a while to climb, mainly because I'm snacking. Besides, I overate on the viperfish and just wanna take a nap. Yawning, I eye a thick ole tree branch rich with sun blossoms. Nah, I'm too lazy to climb the tree. I think I'll just scratch the itch on my flank and maybe nap down here.

As I approach the tree, something offensive disturbs my senses. I pause and lower my nose to the ground, scenting. The Ra. Their territory, their stink. Yuck. Which reminds me, I shouldn't scratch on a tree and leave my scent here. Ark, the Ra's stupid Alpha, would think I'm trying to mark his fucking tree and start a war over my itch.

I move away from it and continue searching for the womankind's camp. Sounds that don't belong in the forest direct me, and I follow the loud stomping. Even barefoot, womankind bang the ground. They're some of the strangest prey I've ever encountered.

Hm. What's this? I sniff the ground. Oh hey, she marked the Ra territory. It's still wet. Didn't even dig a hole to hide the scent. Ark would have an aneurysm. I smile. Whatever displeases Ark makes me happy.

I move along and lie on my belly to watch her in the clearing. The female is stepping into the awkward clothing her kind wears at the bottom to cover their two holes. Not panties. These are called pants. Dark blue, large, and ugly pants, which she fastens with a leather belt. Why, oh why? It will take forever to remove the garment just to waste.

Shaking my head, I circle the clearing she's claimed as hers. A Ra campground, no doubt from the wars. I see the bones of my tribemates as I pass, ripped hunter pelts here and there. It reeks of Ra, and my aggression only rises, their scent irritating my nose.

Suppressing a growl, I circle around and creep behind her so she can't see me. She definitely can't hear me. Unlike her species, we are stealth predators. Besides, human hearing isn't as good as ours. She's still prey. Pretty, but prey. If I were hungry... Good thing I already ate.

Pausing behind the pod, I sling off the sack, and the transition into male flows through my body, taking only a moment. I note that my muscles bulge more than usual. I flex my biceps and smirk. I've always been the best-looking male in the Ka tribe, and after consuming viperfish, I'm also most fit. The goddess's gonna be falling at my feet.

But first I need to figure out how to approach her and not make her wanna take off in the pod. I need her to trust me and warm up to me during the time I erect another portal. It'll take a few spans, no less, because this is Ra territory, and any of our portals in their territory must remain hidden.

Making sure I'm well-dressed in my best verto, I leave my weapons near the sack and fix my hair, both on my head and face, flex my arms, abs, and thighs. Fitness at optimum, I round the clearing so I'm not sneaking up behind her. Before showing myself, I take out my gift. It's a gold-dipped hairclip in the shape of a flower, matching the color of her hair—and mine, for that matter. I smile, bottom lip covering the sharp edges of my upper teeth.

I'm a friendly predator, no?

CHAPTER FOUR

TATYANA

A tall male with long sun-kissed hair steps out of the forest. He wears a kilt with jewelry dangling across it. In his palm, he carries something that he holds out toward me. His white eyes make me uneasy but he's smiling. He's humanoid. He seems friendly, so it must be one of the warrior species that patrol Joylius. *I'm going home.*

At first, I don't believe my eyes. I blink multiple times as I stand, dropping the wood I've been carving out of boredom. I wipe my hands on my pants. "Are you really here?" I ask.

He takes another step forward.

Tears gather in my eyes. A flood of emotions overwhelms me, and I run to him, fling myself at the male. I bury my face in his neck and laugh-cry at the same time. "Oh my God, thank you for coming. I'm so relieved. Oh my God, thank you. Thank you." I cling to him for dear life. This male is a lifeline. *I'm going home.*

I haven't touched or spoken to or seen another human or humanoid alien in what seems like a year, and I'm starved for a conversation and even touch. He's gonna take me home!

The male's chest vibrates on my breasts, and I hear a

muffled sound I can't identify. I step back and wipe the tears off my face. "Sorry for attacking you," I say, though I'm really not. "It's been a while since I've seen anyone, and I'm a little excited." When he says nothing, it takes an effort to keep my gaze locked on his face. His body is…mind-blowing. "I can't believe you found me," I continue. "I'd hoped someone would, but you know that little voice at the back of my mind saying nobody is coming kept getting louder and louder as the days turned into weeks."

I wait for him to reply, but he remains silent and offers me a pretty hairclip.

I accept and secure my bangs away from my forehead with it. "That's really sweet. Thank you." I try not to blush as I give in to temptation and take in his body. Hot damn, these alien warriors are good-looking. His abs put Jackson's abs to shame, and Jackson is a dancer that swimmers wish they looked like. There's edges on this male's jaw. He's tattooed and wears wood and gold beads in his hair. A Viking that could plunder all night long. Okie dokie, then, that will be all. I need to carry on.

"I'm Tatyana," I say and twirl my hair. Jesus. Clearing my throat, I extend my hand. Frowning, he stares at my hand and speaks for the first time. I understand nothing. Odd. I thought any warrior-class beings our National Security hired would have translators.

I run two fingers over my throat and touch my lips. "Your translator is not working," I say. At initial contact with another species, we speak English first, so that's what he should've done. "Russian, maybe?" I prompt him in my native tongue, which sounds odd even to my ears. I haven't spoken Russian since my mother died.

The man—male—reaches behind his kilt and steps closer. I remain in place, even though his movement, fluid and fast, makes me uneasy. His massive presence makes my heart beat faster, and I can't quite discern if I'm excited or scared. Excited, likely, as fear is unjustified. He's gonna get me home.

He sniffs my hair and stands there, my shoulder touching his chest. Is this some sort of greeting I should know about? I've never met a warrior alien. Most humans haven't. Extenuating circumstances call for extenuating behaviors, I guess.

So I sniff his hair. Oh girl, he smells like the ground after rain, heavy and spicy. He's a cockfest, especially after my five-year abstinence.

What can I say? Men have a way of breaking my heart. It's not them, really. It's me. I always fall for the liar. Lesson learned multiple times, I stopped dating and focused on my last years at the LA Ballet.

I'm turning forty-two soon, and I'm tired of wasting time on the wrong guys. If I'm being honest, I'm ready to retire my pointe shoes. I trained another prima to take my place, and the solo performance on Joylius might have been my last one. I hadn't decided yet, but I did hope to see some apartments on that planet far from Earth and its current politics with Mars.

The male speaks again, and his voice at my ear sounds like he's playing a cello, strong and masculine, and I want to be the violin he overpowers. Something stings my temple, and I wince, rubbing the place, but feel no bump or anything there. Fucking bugs in this place, I tell ya. They're the size of birds.

The male taps my shoulder, and I turn to see him towering over me, hot smile still in place. He's cute in a boyish way, albeit with edged cheekbones. I wonder how old he is. Half my age, I bet. Before I hump his leg, I step away.

"Speak to ascertain your translator is working," he says in a language spoken from the chest and the back of the throat.

Oh. The sting was a translator. "I thought you were supposed to wear those."

He shakes his head.

Weird. Joylians wear translators. Humans don't. I presumed warriors in our alliance would also wear them. "It works, and as a bonus, I'm ready if you wanna get moving today."

He frowns.

Facepalm. "I'm sorry. I'm... I'm eager to leave, and you must be tired, scouting the forest for me. I've had a chance to view the terrain, and I'm so grateful you're better at this than I am, because I couldn't have found me, if that makes sense. Here." I point at the firepit area, which has logs placed nicely around it so people can gather and converse. "Have a seat. I have some tea I've been making from plants that are safe. Would you like some?"

"Um..." He scratches his head. "Where do you think you are?"

"That's the thing. I know only parts of Joylius and have no idea where exactly I landed, but only that the pods land on the target location. Are we far from the capital?" I swat my hand through the air. "Stupid question. I'm rambling. I'm sorry. We must be far from the mainland, or you would've found me sooner." He sits down, and I sit across from him.

"I'm surprised you came on foot," I say.

"This is a restricted airspace."

"Oh, I didn't know, and I've been flying back and forth from the beach. Hm, does that mean we're gonna leave my pod behind and go on foot?"

"Something like that." He scrubs his face, then leans on his elbows. The movement makes his biceps flex. "Where do you think you're going?" he asks.

Good heavens, those arms are big. The shoulders, the muscles, are so well defined. Even his tendons show as lines holding all that hotness together. Heat crawls up my face, and I giggle. I haven't blushed in ages. It feels kind of good, so I roll with it.

"Female, where you do think you're going?"

Shit. He's talking to me, isn't he? "To the capital, of course." I frown. Maybe I'm asking too much of this one male. "That's my eventual destination, but I'm very happy to follow you to the nearest safe place where National Security can pick me up and clear me for the flight back to Denver. Earth, I mean." Does he know of Denver? I wonder. We know nothing about these aliens, only that they exist and that we're in alliance with them against the common enemy somewhere in space, or even Mars, judging by the recent developments between the two human colonies. Humans on Mars seem to want to suffocate the rest of us who stayed behind, but that's a political debate I won't start with the warrior who's come here to rescue me.

He strokes his neatly braided beard and purses his lips. They're the only soft part of him. Plush. Smooth. And his muscles flex and relax as he strokes the beard first, then the back of his neck, clearly showing me his biceps and the side of his torso. There are muscles there I've never seen on a man, and I've danced with some amazing partners. This is a whole other level of man. This is a *male*.

I grab the leaf I use to drink water from and fan myself. It gets hot out here midday.

The male pauses and wiggles his nose in a very inhuman way. "My fitness pleases you," he says with a wink.

I am way too old to play coy. "It does," I admit.

"You're welcome to look, female."

I chuckle. The boy—and he's definitely younger than me by at least a decade—sure is assertive. I like that quality in a man. Makes me feel like he's confident and will handle things. "I'm so relieved you're here. I know I keep saying that, and I can talk a lot sometimes, or most times, but I really am relieved. You just rest up a bit and then tell me when and where, and I'll be ready."

"Sounds good," he says.

I smile. What a nice alien. I have no idea why shacking up with warrior aliens is taboo on Earth. Again, I'm way too old not to follow my pussy. I wink back at him.

CHAPTER FIVE

MAS

The female believes she crashed on the vacation planet of her original destination. I can see how she mistook the Blood Dunes for a tropical paradise. It makes me wonder...if their National Security ever discovered Nomra Prime, would they make this area a tourist place?

Ark would never surrender a Ra territory to an invader, but if he did, it would be wonderful to watch human blood spilling on the sand day in and day out until they figured out something's wrong with the place. Eme walked the sand, and all who do now bleed on it. If this is Eme walking again, blood will spill.

She's even prettier up close than from afar. There're sun spots over her nose and cheeks that make her appear younger, though I believe she's a bit older than I. More ripe for the taking, and definitely at the breeding age where she could give me a litter of pups after only one breeding.

I growl. *What the fuck am I thinking?* I slap myself.

The female's eyes widen. "Is everything okay?'

"Fine, female. All is fine." I stand and rub the back of my neck. I hadn't expected her to believe she's on a friendly planet that humans have colonized, and I definitely hadn't expected her to welcome me as she has. I expected the worse, actually. That I'd find her remains. In case I found her alive, I planned to feed her and have a chat with her, explain we are in enemy territory and I'll get her out of here soon. Depending on how she took the news that she wasn't on Joylius, I'd go from there. I definitely hadn't planned to tell her, people classify me and mine as predators. That seems to freak them out, and freaking her out isn't something I want to do.

I'm still gonna work on the portal, and while I do that, she needs to do something else other than follow me around. But I have to explain why we're not leaving. She expects a rescue mission, and I'm here to lure her in, make her less resistant, more likely to follow me into the portal.

Hmm. She enjoys my fitness. I peek down at the verto tent made by my dick. My fitness likes her back. The Ka know what it's like not to have any contact with a female, not even a mother. It makes us all a little too eager and a bit too forceful, like Hart and Nar. I'm not gonna be forceful or eager. I have self-control even when faced with a pretty female I believe is a fierce goddess who wants to bleed me. But she is also grace. All fucking grace. The way she moves her body even when not dancing... I could watch her forever.

The need to slap myself again rises, but I suppress the jerking reaction because it might make me look like I'm crazy.

The female moves back to the pod and returns with a backpack. She's ready, round blue eyes wide and hopeful. I'm gonna feel bad squashing all that hope, so I better make up for it with my dick.

She'll like my dick. Biggest in the tribe. I need to explain why we're not leaving now or anytime this span or the next.

Thunder strikes in the distance, and the female jumps,

pacing a hand over her heart. "Shit, it's gonna rain." She searches the sky. Dark clouds gather and block the sun almost immediately, and I blow a kiss for Aoa, goddess of thunder, the patron goddess of the Ka tribe and my best friend's marked mate. Which reminds me... I reach into my pocket and take out the medicine.

The female approaches and stares, then looks up, pretty, long light eyelashes blinking over those mesmerizing eyes. I've never seen eyes the color of the seas, and they trap me as I stare into them.

"Those are my iron supplements," she says.

I nod and step closer, sniffing her hair again. She doesn't step back. I'm surprised and pleased she doesn't fear me. I'm gonna turn her in for the games and guard her while I master the terrain with portals my tribe hasn't yet seen. I can't stand other people touching my fucking controls. They could fuck them all up, and I'd have to spend a turn on untangling the webs, loose ends, and spatial openings that could dump them out in the middle of the seas for all they know. And if the Ra attack while my portals are malfunctioning, it could mean death to us all. It happened once before, and I won't let it happen again, not while I'm the portal master. Amateurs don't get to touch my controls, and sure as fuck they don't run games in the Ka tribe.

"Where did you find them?" she asks about the medicine.

"In another pod."

"My pod!" She thrusts her fists in the air. "You found my pod. Did you get the violin?"

"I don't believe so."

"That's too bad. She was a favorite. Eh..." She swats at the air, but stays close to me, our bodies almost touching, her nipples almost poking my chest.

She is so pretty. So very pretty, and a purr rises in my chest at the same time as her lips part and red colors her cheeks. I bend my head slightly, tilting it. "I'm going to taste you," I tell her. "And if I do, there's a chance I won't stop. You see, female, I've never tasted a womankind, and you smell yummy."

She rises on her toes and, because she's tall for a female, closes the distance, then pecks my lips, blue eyes wide and expressive, practically twinkling with mischief. She's a goddess, this one. Takes what she wants. Gonna leave me all twisted in my head. It will be worth it. Her body, her pussy on my dick, will be so worth the madness and the eventual loss, the heartbreak I'll suffer. Eme belongs to no one predator.

"Thank you for the pills, warrior."

"Mas," I say. "My name is Mas."

"Mas."

It's as if she said *taste me*. I grab the back of her head and growl as I kiss her, pushing my tongue into her mouth and savoring the womankind. Finally, I understand what's gotten Hart and Nar into marking and breaking all the rules in the lands. She tastes like sweet liquid blood at the back of the throat, a fresh meal, the heart of prey, the softest sweetest part of flesh, and I twirl my tongue, bending her at the waist, wanting to devour her.

She hooks her long leg over my hip, and I grab the back of her thigh and lift, pulling her closer, pressing her against my cock so she can experience the fitness that awaits her when I fuck her. Kneeling, I take her down with me. Her blunt fingers rake my scalp, and I scent she's drawn blood before she fists my hair and growls into my mouth. I growl back and part my verto, then grab my cock.

Thunder strikes the firepit in the camp.

Rain pours over my back.

The female lets go of me and blinks as if waking up from a daze.

I shake off the rain. I hate getting wet. I hate Ra territory. Can't even fuck for the first time in my life in peace. Pissed, I snarl and leap off her. On the ground, face turned up, she closes her eyes. "I have no idea what came over me, but it was inappropriate."

To help her up, I extend a hand, and she takes it. "No, it wasn't."

She chuckles. "It's definitely inappropriate where I come from."

"Luckily, your geolocation has changed." Forever. You just don't know it yet.

CHAPTER SIX

TATYANA

The warrior male I almost fornicated with walks away. I gather my wits and note the rain has stopped as suddenly as it started. The clouds practically disappeared, and the sunrays are breaching the trees again. Humidity has risen in the span of a minute, making the ground smell stronger, heavier. Like the male I just made out with. A male of another alien species.

Even though I'm okay with it, it's something I'll be keeping to myself for the rest of my life. Alien species and humans don't mix, and I feel dirty not only for what happened but because I liked it and feel totally unapologetic about it, even though I tried to sound apologetic when I said it was inappropriate.

Mas sure knows how to make out. Forceful but not painful. Just how I like it.

Standing, I'm dusting off my ass when Mas says from behind me, "I found something else in your pod. But before I give it to you, I need to emphasize I found it and do not know to whom it belongs if it's not yours. Are we clear on that?"

"Sure." I nod and tuck my hair behind my ears. On the ship bound for Joylius, I used the bathroom and never made it back to my seat. When the captain announced an emergency and the ship started tumbling, I secured myself on the first seat close to me. A man's seat, judging by the clothes in the backpack. Hence, my iron pills stayed in my luggage along with all my luggage.

The male holds up my red thong.

"Nice find. Yup, those are mine."

"Going good for me so far," he mumbles. "I have more things." He reaches into his sack and pulls out my flip-flops, my casual blue dress, my bra, even my purse, and I dig inside to find my lip gloss. I put it on immediately and smack my lips, reveling at the watermelon taste. "This is awesome." In the pod, I change into my clothes, feeling like I've somehow returned to my old self. I'm definitely ready to head back home.

Mas is dragging something dark green out of his sack. After dropping the thing, he starts shoving large nails into the ground.

"Can I help?" I ask.

He tosses me one end of the massive green cloth. "Hook the white strings on the nails," he says.

I do and so does he, then he stands back. I do the same.

"All hooked?" he asks and winks.

I wink back. "Yup."

He pulls a string, and a tent pops up in the clearing.

I round it to get to Mas on the other side. Standing before him, I search his inexpressive white eyes for an explanation. When he offers none, I ask, "Why do we need a tent?"

"Because we're not leaving today."

I curl my toes, go to tuck my hands into my pockets, then remember the dress has no pockets. "Why not?"

"It's too late to cross the forest in sunlight."

"We have a pod. Halfway with the pod, then the rest on foot?"

Mas shakes his head. "That won't work."

I sigh. "Tomorrow, early in the morning, then?"

"A few spans at least."

All hope dies, and I panic. "You don't understand. I've been stuck here forever, and when you came, I thought we'd be leaving, and now you're telling me I have to wait a few more days. And you know what else? I saw a massive hell horse with teeth the size of my thumb kill an anaconda from hell, so I'm not really keen on staying anymore. Can we please leave sooner? Maybe before I completely lose my mind? I've tried not to talk to myself, but believe me, it's becoming harder and harder with each passing day. And I just can't—"

Mas's arms come around me. He presses my cheek to his chest. "Shhh. You're in distress and becoming hostile. Calm down."

I wind my arms around his waist and enjoy his touch as his fingers run through my hair. I sigh. "Deep down," I whisper, "I have this…knowing that tells me I'm never leaving this place. I want to be wrong about that."

He purrs, as in really purrs, a deep, rich masculine purr at my ear. He's trying to be kind while I'm freaking out.

"I wish we'd leave now. I so want to leave now, put this place behind me."

"This is not a friendly territory," he says. "There are things in the forests you humans aren't aware of. Because of that, I need to prep our exit with some of the…the technology my people have and your people don't. In a few spans, instead of crossing all the terrain, we will simply appear at your final destination."

I lift my head. "How?"

"Via a portal."

Oh wow. "You mean like a spatial opening from here to the final destination?"

"Yes."

"No walking required?"

He smiles down at me. "A few steps."

"I thought portals existed only in fantasy books."

"Not sure what that means."

"Get out."

"I'm not inside, female." He smiles. "But I will be soon, and getting me out is gonna be the last thing on your mind." He spanks my bottom, then grips it. "Are you done stressing now?"

I chuckle. "You're a naughty boy."

"Thirty-one full turns make me a mature male."

"I'm forty-one," I say. "And in my experience, male maturity is reached at sixty plus." I wink.

He squeezes my bottom. "Where I come from, a female of your age has a ripe womb that can sustain an entire litter, not just one or two pups."

I form an O with my mouth. What an awkward phrase for babies. His species sure is interesting.

Mas releases me and continues working on the large tent.

"Looks like I'll at least get a good night's sleep," I say.

"I doubt that, female." He laughs.

God, I'm happy to have him here. He's easy on the eyes and body, and makes me feel like he could handle anything. There's an aura of self-confidence about him, especially in the way he converses with and approaches me.

Men have never approached me with such ease. Most I intimidate, either because of my looks or my brains, and when they find out people pay to watch me perform, most men get jealous and possessive. They start bickering about the male dancers and cause me performance problems. One such was my ex. He's in jail for beating me now, but it took me nearly dying to put him there. Putting a senator away takes a ballerina walking up to the stage at the Super Bowl halftime show in bruises and with a broken arm.

I did it, and I don't regret a thing. Too bad I didn't summon the courage to do it sooner. George, my performance partner, didn't survive the beating he took on his way home one night. My ex's hired muscle left him for dead in an alley, and days after the senator's arrest, George passed away in the hospital. He was gay, so we never had a thing. But that's not all. He was only nineteen and the most masculine yet graceful dancer I'd had the pleasure of working with. Like Mas, he was strong and confident, and I trusted him on the lifts.

"Hey, can I ask you something?"

"You can ask me anything, female."

The female address sure is sexy. "You familiar with the animal life around here?" Wanting to help set up the tent, I extend my hands. He passes me a bundle of furs I presume is the bedding. I walk into the large tent and search for the best place to put the stuff.

Mas walks in behind me and to the partition in the tent. He points. "In here. And yes, I'm familiar with the local animal life. Why?"

I drop the furs inside the partition. "Because I'm curious about the thing that I refer to as a hell horse."

"I'm unsure that's what you saw."

I show him my teeth and make the most vicious face I can summon, then snap my teeth near his throat. "Huge teeth. Orange eyes. Thick golden fur. Massive. Size of a horse and can take down an anaconda. Also from hell."

Mas smiles. "An impressive beast."

"Definitely. I'm a little more apprehensive now. Sleeping in the tent out here with that thing out there. It didn't look friendly."

"The hell horse is friendly."

"Are you sure?"

"Mmhm. You can pet him." Mas exits, and I follow him back outside.

"How do you know it's a boy horse?"

"Because there are no girl *horses*."

"What do you mean?"

He hands me an ax.

I grip it, and it drops like a log. "Damn, that's heavy."

Mas picks it up and twirls it in his hand. "I mean what I said. There are no girls of his kind. All dead now."

"Oh no. That's sad. Is the animal going extinct?"

"Near extinction."

"That makes me sad. What are the locals doing to help?"

"They're finding other species to breed him with."

"Great. I like hearing that."

Mas sighs heavily. "Yeah." He scrubs his face and curses, then peeks at me from between his fingers.

"What?" I ask.

"Nothing." His hand falls away from his face, and he shudders visibly. "Can you tell me what you've been eating all this time?"

"Mainly small animals. I needed the meat."

Mas frowns. "How are you getting the animals?"

I snort. "The hard way. Hiding until they come, and then, if I'm lucky, I catch one."

Mas smiles. "You've been hunting."

"Sort of. Yes."

He presses a fist to his mouth and tilts his head. "Do you like hunting? Maybe bleeding it slowly and drinking their blood?"

Some days when I felt fatigue creeping up, I bled them and drank the blood. I don't tell him that, though. I swallow, shaking my head in denial, wondering if he's been watching me the entire time or if he's also weird about hunting. "That would be weird, so no."

"Weird or not, have you done that?"

"I'm iron deficient. If I hadn't drunk the blood and hunted, I would have died. I couldn't allow myself to get to the point of fatigue. I'm sorry if this sounds savage to you, but I did what I thought gave me best chance of survival."

Mas seems to adjust his crotch as if all this is making him aroused. Something orange and black lurks behind the white of his eyes.

I step closer to see better, and he lets me. "You have pupils," I say. "Vertical pupils."

"Where do you leave the prey you don't consume? Bones maybe, or leftover flesh?" he asks, voice mangled and animalistic sounding. This warrior species might look humanoid, but they definitely aren't. It's a bit scary, but I'm not afraid of Mas. In a way, he's my hero.

"I'll tell you if you tell me something and not lie."

He nods, and I continue. "Have you been watching me?"

He appears as if he has to think about it, and my face drops. "How long have you been watching me?" I press.

"Only since before I walked into the campground."

"Are you lying?"

He shakes his head.

"Okay, yes, I have a place where I prep the animals. Not here 'cause of the smell, you know. Oh hey, are you hungry? Is that why you're asking if I have leftovers?"

"Starving."

"Oh! Ooo, I'm sorry I haven't offered you anything." I wind my arm under his elbow and lead him a few miles away from the camp. We step onto a path in the forest, and Mas stops moving. I nudge him, but he won't budge. He unwinds my arm from his and steps away, gaze on the massive old tree in the clearing with animal leftovers at the base.

"Bones were here when I found the tree. I figured it's a resting place so I added mine to it." I wince. I've never hurt a fly before, and the guilt eats at me, but I had to eat.

Mas blinks. "You've hunted, then brought prey here and left some of it under the tree."

"Like I said. It seems to me that the people who set up the campground did that, so I just did whatever I thought they'd done." I walk to the skeleton on the ground. "This is old. Someone was already doing this. All I did is follow along since I didn't really know what I was doing in the first place."

"Do you not see what this place is?"

"Some sort of burial ground, I presume."

"Nah-ha." Mas shakes his head and keeps moving away.

Something's freaking him out. "Okay, well, I'm sure you can hunt for yourself." Fuck his judgment. I stomp off. "You asked how I've been surviving, and now I feel terrible about it, as if I didn't already."

"Female," he calls after me.

I spin. "Some of them were here already. They look ancient. Can't you see that?"

"Exactly! Which is why no male in the lands would ever come near this place." Mas shudders.

"Near which place? What do you mean?"

"We're on Herea's hunting grounds." He points back where we came from. "This is a sacrificial path leading to the altar. The tree. Half for the hunter, half for the goddess."

"Who is Herea?"

"Goddess of the hunt and harmony."

"Oh." I walk back to him. "A pagan goddess. That's neat. You know, I wondered if some sort of Joylius tribe lived around here. It looked like they might, but nobody ever came, so I assumed they left for the season. Maybe migrated, yet to return."

"Female, no tribe lives here."

"So there are tribes?"

"Mmhm."

"The more I discover about this part of Joylius, the more I like it. Tell me everything. I want to hear more."

"Shhhh." He presses a finger over his mouth and looks around, eyes wide. He seems afraid. "Herea is not to be roused. Ever." He shakes his head vehemently.

Oh, okay. I whisper, "Why not rouse her?"

"Because she hunts...the hell horses."

"Nooo."

He nods.

"That's terrible. She must be a fierce goddess, then."

Mas takes my hand and leads me away from the grounds back to the camp. I ask many questions, but he's not quite with me anymore, and so I shut up and walk around the camp, sometimes glancing at him while he sits on the log and stares into space. He seems spooked. And I should be too, and yet, oddly, I feel everything is just as it should be.

CHAPTER SEVEN

MAS

Eme has males already serving her. Because she is a womankind she does not understand. Because womankind carrying goddesses within them is unexpected, the males serving her will not understand. But I do. A drained headless body of a male Ra hunter hanging from a tree told me the Ra have already sacrificed one of their own.

I'm starting to put together the pieces of what's happening here. The Ra scent around the camp, though old, isn't ancient, and while the Blood Dunes and the surrounding forest as well as this mountain are considered their territory, if Herea were to walk again, I presume she would come here and claim this land for herself. She might have already, and I haven't found her yet. Or I have found her, but have mistaken her for Eme.

Shuddering, I move to the tent and take out the second leather pouch the Sha-male packed for me. I empty it on the fur and scrub my face, as if that can erase the images I witnessed. An entire path of sacrifices for Herea. I hope that's not who this womankind is.

While Herea is the most popular goddess in the lands

because she is the goddess of the hunt, she's unwelcome in the tribes for she controls the hunters. They're her pets, and while I joked about Eme petting me if she saw me in hunter, I regret it now.

This entire place starts to make me itchy all over, makes my hunter edgy. I scratch my chest, arms, thighs. It's an itch that won't go away. I know what this is. Many of my ancestors experienced it around Herea and her daughter Eme.

I need to leave this place as soon as possible, which means I need to get working on the portal and not sniff up the goddess's pussy. My dick jumps as if it knows something's about to get up on him. Or down. I want to hold her down, press her into the dirt, and fuck her until she screams herself voiceless.

"Mas?" Eme whispers from the other side of the tent flap.

I grab my balls and squeeze hard. The pain shoots up my belly, and I bend over, eyes about to pop out of my head. "Yes?" I squeak out.

"Are you dressed? Can I come in?"

I whisper back, but she can't hear. "Eme, my sweet, blood-thirsty Eme, you can come in even if I'm not dressed. Especially if I'm not dressed." I bet Eme fucks like wildfire. I bet she can't be tamed in bed. I bet Eme would want to mount my dick and ride me. Oh, Herea. I slap myself. I can't even call up Herea or swear on her anymore. Goddesses are everywhere!

"Mas?"

In a single sweep of my hand, I gather up the Sha-male's items and put them back into the pouch, then walk to the flap and open it. Eme's tied her hair in a high bun, and she's got a bag over her shoulders again.

"Going somewhere?" I ask.

"Moving into the tent." Eme squeezes past me and wiggles her eyebrows as the front of her body brushes mine. That's not all. She stops and presses herself against me and undoubtedly feels my erection. "You know that humans don't mix with other species, right?" she whispers.

They mix, all right. Back during Gur's games, Nar's Aoa mixed with him. I suffocated from the smell of her sweet pussy in the tent that one night I slept with them while my wounds healed. It was all I could do not to steal her from him. Womankind smell so sweet, it is alluring, teasing all my senses.

And I'm stuck alone with Eme. Eme, who was taken out of Herea by Bera's own two hands, blessed with fertility, born irresistible to both the hunter and the male. Hunter wants to hunt for her and become her little pet, and the male wants to fuck her whenever she feels like it. Eme is also a pack goddess, meaning she takes multiple males at once. Eme wasn't satisfied with one male. Her two holes were filled at once. I'm gonna need an extra dick, because I sure as fuck don't share.

Of course, I'm not sharing. Or fucking. "I'm going to work on getting us out of here."

"Take your time," she whispers.

Why is she whispering? It's sexy and cute and I can't stop the movement of my head when it lowers and I peck her lips. She tilts her head and lets me kiss her, moaning into my mouth again. I can't stop myself from wanting to touch her. Everywhere. I grab her ass with both hands and squeeze, then lift her and walk over the partition to grab some fur. Using my foot, I lift a pelt and toss it on the floor. I put Eme on the floor and point. "Stay here."

She giggles. "Okay."

"I'm gonna erect the dick, and we'll be on our way."

She laughs.

"The *portal*." I knock on my head. "I'm gonna erect the portal."

"I'm looking forward to it."

Exiting the tent, I breathe some fresh air and knock on my head again. Wind. There is wind blowing through a vast empty place where my brains used to reside. I look up and close my eyes. "Come on, Mas. It's just a female. A single female. You've seen all of two before and survived, came away with your brain and your dick still with you. You can do this."

I roll my shoulders and step back inside, walking straight for my sack. I get my portable controls and stand in the middle of the tent. Now, the portal gets erected—gonna stop thinking that word in my head—under the cover of the tent where I'm least likely to be seen in case any Ra come around. The chances of the Ra returning to the camp for the female are high. Also, I'm a paranoid motherfucker, and I never ever set up portals in front of other people. Nar gets to watch me lift a portal from thin air. But not many others.

Eme's watching me intently. I feel her gaze on my profile, and she's making me itchy. My balls swell under her gaze, my cock starts oozing semen, and I'm horny up to my brain, which conjures up images of her pussy leaking sweet fluid on my tongue.

"Shut up, Mas," I tell myself and slap my cheek. This works. It always works. Nar and I have been slapping away crazy thoughts since we were kids. All wayward thoughts get slapped. By the time the night is over, I'm gonna end up beating myself to a pulp, but it'll be worth it. Once I get Eme to Kalia, I'm gonna put her on Hart's throne and assume the guardian role in the games, which nobody will dare enter. I'll have to talk my tribemates into entering, unless I don't reveal who I think she is. If I can get away without revealing Eme, I will.

For now, I will not touch Eme anymore. Or kiss her. Or mount her. Cue hook spouting semen that slides down my dick and makes my balls sticky. I wiggle my ass to unstick them, but it won't do. Turning away from Eme, I part my verto and scratch first, then look down at the hook that's hard and red and angry looking, the tip facing me, looking more like a claw ready to hurt my brain if I don't use it soon.

I flick the hook, and the pain zaps my belly. Groaning, I get ahold of myself and bend to swipe the sack off the ground. I rummage inside, searching for the portal base. Where the fuck did I put it? I packed it. Looking around, I find it already on the ground waiting for me.

Winded brain.

Kneeling, I get to work on the root of the portal, not once glancing at Eme.

* * *

Late into the night, I'm still working on the portal when I notice I made another mistake. Third mistake I made since Eme asked if she could light a fire. She's got fur. She'll be fine.

I keep at the portal, arranging spatial disruptions into the order that signals to our laws of nature that it's a portal. I should finish tonight and be able to close and open the portal tomorrow without having to start over.

Under the furs, Eme twists and turns. I'm not watching her, but I sense her discomfort, and it's making me uncomfortable. She expects servitude, and I'm refusing to start the damn fire. I will not be her servant. It's not going to happen. She has fur. She'll be fine.

When she can't seem to settle into sleep, she grabs the furs I intended for myself. From the corner of my eye, I see she's dragging everything out of the sack onto a single bed, which means I'm gonna sleep somewhere in the corner in hunter.

Nope, I can't do that. Not only will the hunter freak her out, but Eme, like her mother, can draw out my hunter and turn him into her pet.

I better work faster.

My hands fly over the tiny dots I'm trying to align with the nearest portal we have on Ra territory that will then communicate with the portal controls in my bedroom and ping back a signal to me, closing the loop and erecting a portal out here. I swipe my hand to the left, pick up a viable spatial distortion visible as a tiny golden dot, and carefully hover it over another dot. I just have to connect them, and I can rest.

"Mas?" Eme whispers.

I drop the dot.

It crashes on a random spatial distortion, and a portal shimmers. I peek into it. Not going to Kalia. This portal only goes to the other nearest secret portal I've set up in the Ra territory. I can't close it. I can't open it. It's stuck as it is, and tomorrow, I'll have to untangle the connection from the existing portal without damaging the portal over near Loma. Fuck!

"Mas, can I tell you something?"

"Sure, Eme, tell me whatever you like."

She's quiet, and I curse and turn toward her. "Yes?" I prompt her.

She smiles, a little sad. "My name is not Eme. It's Tatyana."

Not on this planet. "The way you roll letters off tongue to produce words don't roll off our tongues in the same way. We prefer shorter names and phrases."

"People call me Tanya for short."

"I'm gonna call you Eme."

"Oh." She chuckles. "I thought you mistook me for another girl."

"Unlikely." There are no other girls. For me. Maybe there will be one span, when I don't have other things to do, goddesses to worry about, and rescue, and competitions to run, or a tribe to save in case the Ra decide to occupy us again.

"Anyway, what I was gonna say is it's getting late. If you made a mistake, and I think you did, it's a sign you're tired. Sometimes when I dance for hours, I chip my nails, break a toe or two, even, and they bleed and I ignore it 'cause deadlines and perfection. But let me tell you, dancing or working for hours on end makes us more prone to mistakes."

"Female, I do not tire."

"Everyone tires."

"That's because they're unfit."

Eme sits up, a dangerous glint in her eye. "Since you're so fit, then you won't have a problem practicing with me tomorrow."

"I'll be finishing up the portal, and we're leaving tomorrow."

"I practice every morning, come rain or shine. And I could use a partner."

"No way."

She lies back down. "Maybe you're not as fit as you think you are."

"Or maybe you've never seen the very definition of fit."

"And I never will if you don't show me."

CHAPTER EIGHT

TATYANA

Flirting with the sexy warrior is more fun than I've had in ages. He doesn't drop overused or plain dumb pickup lines, and I respect a man who works long hours, makes mistakes, gets up, and tries again. Besides, I've been alone and lonely for a long while, not just the time I've spent on this tropical paradise.

My practice hours run long, and my schedule is packed. When I'm not dancing, I'm training dancers or working either for charity or media or both if I can, which doesn't leave me many hours in the day for pleasure. The starvation for human contact shows now that I'm alone with a man.

Mas takes a pair of axes and twirls them in his palm before flinging them behind him to land on the log he'd brought in earlier. He gets a couple of knives and holds them both in one palm and flings them at me. I scream as they lodge on either side of my body, trapping my hands under the pelt. Wiggling, I can't get out when he flings two more knives, and now my upper body is stuck under the pelt.

"What are you doing?" I ask.

"We're gonna dance, Eme." He unsnaps the belt holding

his kilt, and it hits the ground at the same time as the kilt drops a few inches, stopping right above his pubic area, where it's held up by the bulge under it. "We're gonna dance until one of us tires."

I swallow. Mas has a sharp V of well-honed muscles, and I'd bet my left tit there're dimples on his ass. "Well, go on, then," I say, trying to sit up, then remembering he restrained me. My nipples perk as the pelt rubs them through the thin shirt I wore as my pajamas.

Mas unties the lone remaining string on his kilt, and the material falls away, revealing a perfect penis the size of which no human man could replicate. It's long, wide, veined, and it slowly starts lifting from the down position into a full erection. It moves back down and up like a lift at Mas's will. He's showing he has control of all his muscles, including the one most men can't quite control.

Pressure develops in my belly, and my channel spasms, protesting the emptiness.

In an inhuman way, Mas moves his nose left to right. "What a sweet scent."

I think he's talking about my arousal.

Mas purrs, and something red emerges at the top of his cock. My eyes widen, but I hide the surprise as quickly as possible. I won't disrupt the moment. I want that massive cock inside me. Between my legs, I pulse, arousal turning into an ache. Mas strokes himself from the base to the top, thumb lingering over the protruding red thing, massaging it, making it spurt semen. His purring turns into a loud rumble, and he reminds me of a big cat hovering over its prey, getting ready to eat it.

He strokes faster and shoots semen on the pelt, then crouches at my feet. I wiggle my bottom and lift it. Mas smirks and slowly removes my pants, leaving me in just my panties. He lowers his head, and a claw traces my wet spot.

Up and down at first, then he pushes inside a bit and circles my entrance. My cotton underwear feels like sandpaper against my sensitive opening. I moan and drop my head back on the furs, then lift my hips. Mas moves the underwear to the side and pauses there.

I stare at the ceiling, and when he touches me, gently, spreading my wetness over my clit, back down, and all the way to my small back hole, I close my eyes as excitement builds in my belly.

A finger pushes inside me, and I gasp at the thickness. He finger fucks me, pushing in and pulling out and curling it up, stroking the place that feels amazing. Adding a second finger, he stretches me slowly, and his purring is all a growl now, sounding animalistic. It turns me on, reminds me I'm letting a male of another species play with my pussy. It's taboo and wrong, and I'm down with taboo and wrong.

Once he has two fingers inside me, I feel the flick of his tongue. It's coarse and rough, and I peek down my body at his head between my legs. He's kneeling, so I also see his back. Perfectly straight and muscular. His biceps shift as he pumps me, and I spread my legs wider, as wide as I can, so he can take any angle he wants. His hands fly to my knees, and he holds them down. He starts making out with my pussy lips, his well-groomed beard rubbing my pussy hole.

He juts his jaw and presses it against my opening while he clamps his lips over my clit and starts sucking. I close my eyes as my head thumps on the fur. I lift my hips. Mas growls, and the sound vibrates through my body and I start moaning loudly as he purrs, making my clit swell more and more, making the pressure in my belly build. I grind my hips against his mouth and beard, the friction feeling amazing, and when he nips at my clit, I come with a silent scream because my body locks as my pussy spasms.

Mas laps me up, long fast strokes of his tongue, and he's

moaning like he's feasting. When I come to, I lift my head to see he's reached for the knives. He releases the pelt, and I sit up with his face still between my legs. I bury my hands in his hair, and he snarls, making my pussy spasm again. He laps at me for a while longer, then lifts his head.

Something bright lurks behind the white of his eyes. I'm so transfixed by it that I don't see the moment he lifts the knife and cuts his bottom lip. Blood wells up and drips onto his beard. My heart thumps in my ears.

I get on my knees now and crawl to him. He spreads his legs wider so I can kneel between them. His large palms are warm over my hips as they hold me. Mas leans in and tilts his head, and I do too, and he kisses me.

His blood tastes unlike the others'. It's both sweet and spicy, like cinnamon and citrus, and he swirls his tongue inside my mouth, one hand in my hair moving my head and twisting it anyway he needs it. He grabs my ass cheek with the other hand and pulls me up so I'm kneeling over his thighs. I fold my legs behind my ass and grab his long shaft. I stroke him, feeling the smooth, hard skin. Mas groans into my mouth, and I rub him faster.

He grabs my wrist and pecks my lips. This close to him, where our breaths meet between us, I clearly see a vertical pupil and orange eyes behind the white. Mas gives my hand on his cock a tug and guides it to my entrance. We position it there, and Mas moves his palm toward my bottom and slaps it. I gasp. He squeezes my bottom, spanks it again. Then the other side. He takes my wrists and holds them at the small of my back. My breasts jut out, and he sucks my nipples, moving from one to the other, twirling his tongue.

My channel clings around the tip of his cock as I sit down, making the head of it enter me. Mas thrusts up from under and holds my body tighter, immobile while he jerks his hips from below, controlling the depth and speed and never quite burying himself all the way inside me. He's teasing me.

We fuck like this until sweat soaks my body.

I come three times, my strength leaving me. Even though he holds me, I can't even keep my spine erect anymore. My head falls back. Mas brings me even closer and now buries his cock inside me to the hilt. I scream and come all over it for the fourth time, stars playing over my eyes, body going limp.

He holds me up and starts moving again.

My eyes roll into the back of my head. "You win," I tell him.

Mas stops moving and releases me, then lays me down on the furs. His eyes blaze orange, vertical pupils a slit, and I'm so tired that I'm diving into sleep, my soul demanding I rest. Mas pecks my forehead, lingers there. I feel like he wants to say something, so I open my eyes in a last-ditch effort to stay awake when Mas lies beside me and tucks me against him, my front to his front, pressing my cheek to his chest.

He purrs. The warmth of his body quickly transfers to mine, and the purr lulls me to sleep.

CHAPTER NINE

MAS

Clever Eme exploited my vanity. I didn't see how she lured me into her pussy trap until I was deep inside said pussy, and by then, I didn't care. Her pussy is warm, wet, tight, and grips my cock way better than my fist does, or both fists, for that matter.

I had to show her my fitness, tire her out before I tired so she would find my fitness suitable for breeding. Let it not be said Mas didn't rise to the fitness challenge, even if it killed him in the end.

She's been up for a while now. Before she left the bedding, she stared at me, ran her blunt finger over the outlines of the tattoos on my neck and chest, even gripped my dick and gave it a few strokes, making my hook swell and want to disengage. It was all I could do to hold back and pretend like I was sleeping so I could witness her while she's unaware I was doing so.

Eme explored my hook. Thoroughly. She rolled it between her fingers until it hardened, and for a moment, I thought it would eject and blow a hole through her belly on the way to her womb. This is why my balls are the size of my fists now. And hard as rocks.

Under the fur, I stroke myself, trying to relieve the pressure while thinking about Eme's pussy on my face and the way she likes to grind herself on my beard. I stick my tongue out and swipe some of her liquid off my beard and bring it back into my mouth. The second I taste her pussy, my balls draw up, and I clench my teeth as I ejaculate into my hand.

My dick keeps jerking, balls pumping seed all over my hand, and I'm fucking drenched in cum. Grunting, I move the pelt over my middle and look down at my still-erect dick. Oh well. At least the pressure in my balls has left. I cross my arms behind my head and stare at the ceiling, swiping my tongue over the cut I made on my lip last night.

Eme bedded males in packs of no less than five at the same time. None could satisfy her or breed her. The hunger for a child to grow inside her turned into a vicious flame, and when she couldn't get pregnant, she blamed the males and ordered them to offer her a sacrifice.

At dawn, they bled to their deaths from wounds they couldn't heal. Therefore, Eme was the first of the goddesses to demand a sacrifice from us. After her, all the others followed suit. It is why we sacrifice animals when we think we've transgressed against the goddesses, or when we seek favors. And if we think we transgressed against Eme or want to pray to her, the sacrifice we must give is another one of us.

Which is why Eme is not a goddess we pray to. Especially not the Ka. Hart, the Kai of my people, would balk at the idea. We are just over one thousand males left.

I better figure out how to deal with her and decide if bringing her to the tribe is even something I wanna do. Perhaps I could keep her here. With me. And never return. Even if Tash, the earl of this territory and Ark's brother, came, I have other things he wants, such as my portal secrets.

I could trade with him for letting Eme and me reside in this territory.

What the fuck am I thinking?

Snarling, I stand and scratch my heavy balls. I stretch before I grab the verto and dress, looking around for my daggers, axes, knifes, finding one knife missing. Great. Eme has my weapon now. I scrub my beard and walk past the portal I fucked up last night. Pausing, I groan at the hideous thing, dreading the work ahead of me.

Outside, the sun blinds me, and I flinch before my eyes adjust.

"Good afternoon," Eme says from the log she's sitting on, using my knife to peel something in her hand. She lifts the knife. "Yours is better than mine."

I nod, not feeling chatty when I just woke up. I sit across from her. Eme tilts her head and stands. Knife in hand, she approaches me as if to sit beside me, and my hunter sniffs out a meal. At the scent of her, saliva pools in my mouth. The scent of both prey and the female I want to breed teases my senses as Eme sits on my lap, small cold toes resting on my thigh. She throws a hand over my shoulder and watches me.

I sniff her hair, lick her shoulder, trying to suppress the instinct to chew on her arm. I'm also hard for her and wanna fuck. Her scent confuses me.

Eme, none the wiser, kisses my mouth. "You heal fast," she says and taps my lip.

Actually, with Eme around, I heal rather slowly. I nod, and because Eme has bathed in the sea, her hair is still wet, hence the reason the conflicting scents womankind project are even stronger. I grab her hair and bring her closer, lick her neck, eyeing the jugular. If I bit down, blood would spurt into my mouth, and I could feed and fuck at the same time.

I leap off the log.

Eme falls off my lap while I step away, eyeing her warily.

She stays down, her eyes wide and...and scared. Her fear draws me in even more. My muscles start relaxing, bones moving under my skin, and my hunter pushes to the surface of my mind. He's drawn to her as if Herea commands him herself. I struggle as I push him back.

Eme, still on the ground, grips her knife. "What is happening to you?"

"I...I..."

Eme starts getting up as if to run.

"No, don't run," I rasp. I sound like someone else, my vocal muscles already in hunter.

Eme stands, her knife aimed at me, her hand shaking. She walks backward toward the pod, and I know I need to give her time and space to escape. Hunger for her flashes through me, and especially because I know her blood will be the sweetest I've ever tasted. Her scent clouds my judgment, consumes me, and I crouch, ready to pounce on her when I hear a growl from the woods.

Pausing, I tilt my head, extending my hearing toward the place I heard a growl. There it is again and advancing quietly. Another set of paws joins the first, and then another. In hunter, the Ra are circling us, and they're growling a warning, telling me to back off from their food. There's at least three of them, and I'm outnumbered.

A twig snaps. Make that four Ra.

I glance up at Eme, who's shaking, still watching me, knife outstretched ready to defend herself.

"Get in the pod," I say.

She blinks. "What?"

"You're in danger. Get in the pod."

"No shit," she says. "You tried to...bite me."

Intent on forcing her into the pod, I lurch at her.

Eme slices across my chest. "Don't come closer, or I'll bury this thing in your heart."

When predators are closing in on the prey, the worse thing I can do is turn my back on them. When hunting, we take a split moment to attack a prey, and while I'm not their prey, she is, and I'm standing between a pack of hungry hunters and their meal.

"Eme, I'm not going to hurt you."

"Ha! I might've believed you yesterday, but you woke up a freak this morning."

"I swear to Herea, I wasn't going to consume you."

"Oh my God." Eme's face becomes so pale, it's as if all the blood drained from it. The scent of her fear spreads on the breeze ruffling the leaves. I'm certain the Ra scent it.

"In the pod, Eme."

Eme stands there, gaping. No words are coming to her, and she's in freeze mode, the easiest mode to hunt. The prey stops in shock, and we get to pounce and eat. When I said this would be easy, this isn't what I had in mind.

I sense the Ra closing in behind me. I hear them, so I can mentally place their positions and when one steps into the clearing, I snatch the knife out of Eme's hand and throw her into the pod. Eme stumbles inside but catches herself. Whipping her head around to glance back at me, she narrows her eyes and walks back out to stand before the pod. "What are you going to do?"

I hate having to turn away from her because she is an offended goddess after all, and I have no idea what she might do to me, but I choose to go down trying to protect her from the Ra rather than from myself.

I would have pounced on her. What a fucked-up mess I made. Should've watched Eme from afar while I set up a portal, then simply walked in on her and taken her to Kalia. But no. I had to meet her out here alone and study her a bit, experience the grace of her divine presence all by myself. Well, this Ra pack is gonna teach me a lesson in what happens when I get selfish in wanting Eme for myself and start thinking with my dick.

As if sent here by a goddess, the Ra came just in time. Had they not come, I don't know what would become of Eme. Shuddering, I flip the knife in my hand. Rare is the male who can fight a single hunter and survive. A male fending off four hunters at once is not rare. He doesn't exist. Logically, I deduce I'm gonna die if I don't drop the knife and get on my paws and let my hunter deal with their hunters. In hunter, I'm gonna run. It's a sane decision, and hunters are sane, driven by instinct, and instinct tells him, he shouldn't fight four hunters over food when he's not even hungry.

Eme's still behind me.

I glance back. "Why are you lingering?"

"There are four animals in the camp."

"Hunters."

"Can you fight them off?'

"No."

There's a flicker of movement to my right, and Eme rushes into the tent. One of the Ra snarls, paws throwing back dirt as he readies for an attack. I take stock of the four hunters, assessing their size and demeanor while I back up toward the pod. My back hits it, so that's as far as I can go. The short-haired blond hunter with silver eyes, the one who snarled, appears the largest. He's about my size and leaner, not bulky like Hart or Nar. He's gonna be fast, likely able to fly through the air like an arrow. His back legs shuffle the dirt some more. The others start pacing, growing more restless by the second.

Eme emerges from the tent, her ass up, walking backward toward me, dragging something. She reaches me and steps aside, then drops my ax next to me. "Goodbye, freak, and good luck." Eme lingers, though, her eyes locked with mine. I think she wants to say something, but she swallows and enters the pod. The door closes with a whoosh, and I pick up my ax and twirl it in my hand.

"This is womankind," I say. "Perhaps you've heard of them."

The hunters salivate. They're hungry, and nobody is fucking listening. Though that doesn't stop me from talking, stalling until Eme can fire up the pod. What's taking her so long?

"Womankind are breeders. They smell like food, but they're breeders, and obviously, we're gonna take them as breeders, so I can't let you consume her."

The pack leader snorts, the equivalent of laughter.

I bounce my ax from one hand to another. Eme's certainly gonna get her sacrifice. It's all my fault. I should've never touched her. Eme belongs to nobody, least of all my needy cock.

CHAPTER TEN

TATYANA

The pod won't start. Nervous sweat coats my fingers, and the pod's dash won't respond to a dirty or wet touch. It would if it hadn't been damaged in the crash, but it was, and I'm no expert who could repair it. I discovered the manual controls by accident and learned how to pilot also by accident. And when I say accident, I mean I tumbled down the mountain twice before I learned what to do and kept practicing by piloting this thing daily.

I rub my palms on my blue dress and touch the Start button. It's not working. I scream at it and bang my palm against the dash. It cracks. "Oh no. Oh no." I pat the dash, feeling the cracks under my fingertips.

One animal leaps for the pod.

I cover my head as if it can get to me.

Mas bends at the knees and jumps. He swipes with his ax and roars as he slices across the animal's belly. Blood and guts spill all over him. The other three animals attack, snarling, snapping, bouncing all around him. Mas's trying to fend them off, but the massive hell horses are super fast, biting him as they switch positions.

Mas thrusts his ax at one. Gets his flank. Good.

The animal launches again and bites Mas's calf, taking Mas down to one knee. Mas snarls at them and throws the ax away.

Oh my God, he's gonna surrender and they're gonna rip him to pieces.

I can't watch this. I touch the Start button, gently this time. "Come on, come on…"

A bone in Mas's shoulder juts out, his legs bend backward at the knees, arms twist, and in a second, he's like them. An animal. A hell horse with an orange coat like two of the ones in the campground. They fight in a flurry of snapping teeth, slashing claws, snarls, and blood, and I can't tell if he's winning or not. I no longer care because this is not my fight and Mas hasn't come to my rescue. Mas is a predator-class species who came to consume me. That's what he said to them, and he knew it because he's like them.

I clasp my palms together and lower my head, saying a prayer, and carefully, ever so gently, touch the ignition button. The pod lights up and lifts. The predators fight in a bloody tangle of fur and claws. They sound as vicious as I imagined this species would be. Not that I gave them much of a thought before. They're like the boogie man, the stuff of nightmares nobody has ever seen, and it explains why this area of Joylius remains abandoned.

It also explains how Mas found me. This is their territory. What's worse, I realize as I maneuver the pod away from the campground, is that nobody is coming to rescue me.

I land on the sand. That's as far as the pod will go, and I'm afraid to gun it for the mountain across from the one I've settled on because I've tried before and nearly crashed on the rock when I couldn't find a place to land. An experienced pilot could've landed on the almost-flat rock, but I'm not it, so sand it is.

The bottom of the pod scrapes the sand as I turn it around so I can keep an eye on the campground above, the mountain where predators have gathered for breakfast.

A bloody orange ball of fur leaps out of the trees, followed by two more. He lands on the rock and doesn't linger. Bending those flexible and powerful back legs, he leaps down to the lower rock. They all land at the same time, on the same rock, and the ones chasing him bite his back legs.

His howl of pain makes me wince, and I watch in horror as the orange-coated horse I think is Mas tumbles down, hitting rock after rock, bouncing and leaving blood smears in his wake. The other two pursue. Correction. They stalk him, their heads dipped low, carefully descending, ears pulled back, those giant teeth bloody and exposed. There're no lips to cover the teeth, and bits of flesh as well as tufts of fur from the orange hell horse stick to their mouths.

The orange one falls onto the sand and stays down while the other two descend and lurk at the edge of the sand. One of them stretches out his paw, then pulls it back when his buddy snaps his teeth. On the sand, the orange-coated one doesn't move, but I can see his chest rise and fall. Why aren't they finishing him off? It's Mas for sure, and he's dying, blood pooling on the sand. I know I'm next. Maybe they don't finish off one of their own. Maybe they just took him down and got him out of the way, or maybe he's capitulated like a...a wolf might when faced with a stronger wolf.

In a wolf pack, an Alpha eats first.

I think in all the animal kingdom, this holds true. The loser dies or starves. Which means I'm gonna die or starve out here. They won't leave. I know they won't leave the area the same way I knew Jason wouldn't leave me alone until I put him behind bars. I've always been prey. To men, to managers, to my diet, even to my passions. I've always followed my heart.

Which is why I do what I do next. My stupid heart, bleeding for the injured Mas, nudges me to open the pod door and step outside. It's almost an out-of-body experience, and I might be insane. Maybe I finally snapped. It happens, I hear, to people in isolation and under extreme duress.

Caring nothing for my safety, I cross the sand to the predators. They lift their heads, and their noses move from right to left, the same way Mas has done in his male form.

Saliva starts dripping from the corners of their mouths.

I advance, but not too close. They're fast, but I can still run back to the pod. I can't just watch them tear him apart. He did hold them back for me, even if it was just to defend his own breakfast.

The predators step onto the sand and move toward me. They're snarling and snapping their teeth, but at each other as if talking. I stay in place, my knees shaking violently.

Mas lifts his head. Orange eyes unlike their silver ones blink, and he whines as he tries to get up. He manages to prop himself up on his front legs, but quickly falls to his side. That's when I see it. A chunk of his flank is missing. He's badly hurt. He's not gonna make it.

The predators keep snarling at each other.

Rage builds inside me, and I scream, "Die, you motherfuckers! Die!"

The two predators clash, ripping into each other with fury, all the while whining as if crying and screaming at the same time. I clamp my hands over my ears and watch the dance of death, and before I know how I got there, I'm standing before them. They're dead, bleeding on the sand, blood tickling my toes, running over my foot. I move aside and accidentally step on one's leg. I jerk my leg only to end up treading on the other one's head. I keep trying to escape stepping on them, but I can't. Everywhere I step, I'm landing either on blood or body parts. It's mad and twisted and I don't understand, and because I can't escape the madness, I give up and stay in place. I start crying, snot running down my face.

Mas is sitting up, one leg off to the side at an awkward broken angle. Eyes blazing orange, he simply sits there. I walk to him and spread my arms. "Go ahead and be quick about it."

I expect him to pounce and just snap me in half. End it. I'm tired of this survival shit, and if there're predators here, I'd rather this one kill me fast. The others might toy with me, torture me, take me apart piece by little piece. And I think this one wouldn't do that.

Mas drops to his belly and crawls to my feet, big orange eyes staring up at me. He looks almost like a puppy who got into the garbage and now he's sorry, asking for forgiveness and asking the owner to pet him to reassure him he's forgiven. I sniffle, wipe at my snot, and plop next to the animal, one hand on top of his head. His blood glues my hand to his pelt. "Good boy."

CHAPTER ELEVEN

MAS

The scriptures say Herea often tested her daughters, sometimes for fun, most times to pit the girls against each other and see which one came out the victor. Gentle and graceful Eme never won a single competition, often wiggling her way out of them by faking fatigue or having to work at the local village. Herea thought her weak, at the bottom of the food chain, and sometimes called her a mortal.

One morning, when little Eme went to bathe in the seas, Herea sent a pack of hunters to feed on the daughter she deemed prey. They never returned. Upon hearing that Eme defeated the pack of hunters, Herea sent another pack, and another and another. When none returned, she came herself to watch gentle Eme dance over the corpses of hundreds of Herea's best hunters.

Eme asked her mother why she tried to kill her.

Herea answered, "Because you are weak, and I am only as strong as my weakest daughter."

"Then I suppose you are the strongest now," Eme answered her.

Herea walked away smiling and became the strongest

goddess, and the most popular in all the tribes. Often I wondered how Eme defeated Herea's hunters, and I think I might know now. While the Ra and I fought, our wounds wouldn't heal. Not even small scratches that should have healed instantly, and especially not the chunks of flesh that require longer healing time as it is. When the Ra neared Eme, their wounds opened more, making their blood gush out. Eme drained them dry, their corpses divested of blood and even muscle. Now they are but skeletons on the sands, as if they've been here for turns.

Unlike a male, a hunter knows what's good for him. Sitting next to Eme soothes him, and I'm an idiot for thinking he'd come after her to eat her. He wasn't going to consume her. He was drawn to her, pushing to the surface, wanting her attention. I mistook it for hunger. A rumble breaks from my chest as she pets between my shoulder blades. I purr loudly, lifting the sand in front of my nose.

"You're a predator," Eme says. "And I bet nobody knows. I mean, if they knew predators existed on Joylius, they would have gotten rid of your kind. Or maybe they had hunted you and now you live out here in the middle of nowhere, hiding in the forests. I don't know what to make of you. Are you going to eat me?" She looks down, and I peek up at her, then lift my head.

Saliva drips onto the sand.

Womankind all smell deliciously sweet, and I know they taste sweet, and my hunter has no qualms about drooling over a woman who produces such scents. She teases my senses, my desires, making me more confused than ever. I can't quite think the way I'm used to thinking. Nothing about her is simple. Nothing is easy.

"I'll take your drooling as a yes, then." Eme snorts. "What are you waiting for?"

I lick her ankle. Mmmm. I lick again and up her calf, then

wince as I try to move closer. My snout ends up under her thigh, and I breathe in the scent between her legs.

She flicks my ear. I duck, eyeing her warily.

"What now, Mas?"

In hunter, I heal faster, and when wounded, returning to the male isn't smart. One never knows what additional damage can be caused at the transition stage. I huff out a breath, blowing away the sand in front of me, uncovering a pair of bugs mating. I lift my head.

"Jesus," Eme says. "Those bugs are huge." She scoots back.

I lick my teeth and strike, crunching the snacks to release the sweet sticky liquid from their guts. It explodes in my mouth, and I moan, lapping it up with my tongue. Hart would like these snacks. He's got a sweet tooth too.

"Ew," Eme says. "I can't believe you did that."

Wha… I snort. What else would I do with bugs? Certainly not scoot away. I'm not afraid of my snacks.

The portal on the Dunes, the one I entered through, brightness, signaling an incoming party. I tense and try to sit up but I'm missing a chunk of meat from my flank. Leaning on my better leg, I rise awkwardly, putting more weight on my front legs.

"What's going on? What do you hear?" Eme scoots closer. I lick her face. *It's gonna be okay,* the gesture says. I lick again because she tastes so yummy. I am so confused. I wanna eat her, and I don't wanna eat her. The struggle is terrible. Eme wipes my saliva off her face. "What is it, Mas?"

Nar, my best friend, walks out of the portal, followed by my younger brother, Tis. They scan the area, and because we're farther out and on their right, they don't see us before realizing where they landed.

"Blood Dunes," Nar shouts, and both he and Tis sprint for the rocks.

I roll my eyes. *The tracks. Cover the tracks.* Tis leaps and lands on the rocks, spins around when Nar curses and takes out his ax, and starts running back.

Tis scratches his head. "What the fuck?" he says.

Nar's wiping the tracks with his ax, awkwardly running backward much like I did. I can't stop myself from laughing. I snort, laughter in hunter sounding like I've got pebbles in the throat.

Tis turns toward us, yanking out his daggers.

He probably doesn't recognize me. I'm covered in blood and missing chunks of my pelt.

Nar's made it to the rock and crouches, smiles, carefully taking out his knife. He thinks I'm Ra, and he wants to skin me. Great. Lifting my nose, I howl in a way a Ka hunter would recognize.

Nar straightens to his feet. "If you're not dead, Mas, you better start crawling over here, because I am not walking on the Blood Dunes."

I shake my head. If I move from this place, I'm gonna pass out from the pain, and I don't quite wanna pass out in front of Eme. The endgame was to protect Eme from the Ra. I did that. But the aftermath is still very humiliating. Had they not shown up, I would have spent several spans healing (if possible) and then explaining everything, taken Eme to Kalia, and become a hero for finding another womankind, the one nobody dared bring in for fear of the goddess of blood and grace.

Eme gets up.

No, no. Sit down. I shake my head and whine in protest.

Nar tilts his head. "Sit down, female. Nobody wants to hurt you."

Eme fists the knife and takes off for the pod like there's fire at her heels. Tis curses, and both he and Nar struggle. They crouch to jump, then change their minds because no hunter walks on the Blood Dunes. Not only is it because of legends, but also because we feel bad energy, spirit, whatever coming from this place, and it makes our instincts say *get away from here*.

Which is exactly what Eme is doing. But for different reasons. She gets inside the pod and fires it up. If she takes off, all of this will be for nothing. If she takes off, I have no idea where she'll end up. She's gonna die out there alone. Her home is the Blood Dunes, or somewhere else with me.

I force a transition, tearing out my hip tendons in the process. They snap like cords, causing damage to soft tissues rather than the internal organs near them. A scream tears out of me, and I pant on the sand. Lifting my head, I shout, "You're not on Joylius!"

Eme's made it inside the pod and managed to lift the damn thing without closing the door. It's jammed. These things aren't made for frequent use, and she's been using it to fly every morning since she arrived here.

"If you run, another pack will find you." I say between breaths. The sands start tilting; my head feels heavy. At the corner of my left eye, Tis is emerging from the water, with an arrow tied to a long rope. He nods at me.

I keep talking to distract Eme, who's chosen to hover and listen to me, likely because, despite everything, she trusts that I'll protect her. And lie to her all span long when I have to.

"This is Nomra Prime. We are all predators here."

There's sniffling in the pod. I'm sure Eme is crying. She hung on to hope for so long that it became almost a belief for her, a delusion without which she'd have given up already. It kept her alive to survive the cold nights hunting and dancing. My chest feels heavy for her.

Tis drives the arrow through the dashboard of the pod. The hook releases inside it and latches on, and Nar springs out of the sea. Together, they drag the pod toward them. Eme is screaming, and the sound grates on my ears. I crawl toward the portal and make it there, but my vision blurs as I reach out, half blind, feeling the heat from the spatial opening.

My ears pick up the moment they secure the pod, because Eme's frantic, her screaming desperate, and I close my eyes, wishing I could plug my ears because she's calling my name, thinking I'm gonna save her. Even if I were well, I'd have done the same. I came here to secure a female for my tribe, and I damn well will secure her. A part of me feels as if I betrayed her, somehow, but I'll deal with these strange feelings later, over in Kalia where she'll be safe. Where males will compete for her and she will breed someone cute pups with big, maybe even blue-colored eyes. Or even a female pup. Tall, beautiful, graceful.

Nar grabs my arm and settles under me, groaning as he lifts me. My head swims, and I hold back the contents of my belly as my head hangs. Lifting it, I glare at him, blood seeping between my teeth. "Do not touch my portal."

He gives me the same look I've given him all our lives. The *are you stupid?* look. "Really, Mas? You can't even see the portal."

I stretch out my arm and search the heat spots on the opening, fix one to the left that the hookholes placed wrong, and slump, my weight completely on Nar.

"Are we good now?" Nar asks.

I grunt.

"Moving out, Tis."

Before I pass out, the last thing I see is Tis carrying an unconscious Eme. We're going home.

CHAPTER TWELVE

HART

One of my finest males had gone missing, and we tracked him down to a portal in Ra territory, one I had no idea existed, and I'm mighty pissed he erected a secret portal in enemy territory without telling me about it.

The last time he vanished for spans, he came back with portal access to Mount Omila, a place none of us visit by choice. So it's not the first time Mas has breached another tribe's portal controls, nor is it the first time he's gone off to lands unknown to set one up. It is the first time, however, that I was unaware of his intentions. I cannot have Mas off grid when the Ra in the village near the border are currently picking their earl, since the last earl died. They'll fight among one another and could turn their sights on my territory again.

Whether they'll request a payoff for my brother stealing a female during their games is yet to be seen. Needless to say, I'm in a foul mood, and the last thing I need is a missing portal master, the male who's saved the tribe more than any other by giving us escape routes when we most needed them.

Mas's portal mastery is indispensable to me and crucial to our survival.

Inside Mas's small bedroom from which he runs his portals more often than not, I stand before the portal Nar and Tis entered, hands on my hips, my upper lip curling into a snarl. I might bite Mas on sight. What comes back through the portal makes my blood run cold.

Nar carries Mas's limp body. I steel my jaw so I don't wail in pain when my brother delivers the bad news. Behind Nar, Tis walks into the room carrying a womankind.

I stare at my brother, awaiting bad news.

"He needs the repair system," Nar says.

I swallow. Mas is alive. I take a moment to breathe.

"He needs the repair system, Hart."

"He'll heal," I say. Mas hates the repair system he built. I'm the only predator using it.

"I don't think he's healing, brother."

In disapproval of whatever Mas has done, I shake my head and poke Mas's portal control. Normally, we'd take to the streets to rush him into my chambers under the Hall of the Fallen, but I can't waste a moment because I can barely hear Mas's breathing.

I connect one of his portals with the one in my chambers, and when I see the opening to my room, I walk inside. Nar, carrying Mas, follows me.

"Hey," Tis says from the other side of the portal, still in Mas's bedroom. "What do I do with the female?" He smiles. "Keep her warm?"

"Give her a pelt and leave," my brother barks.

I snap my head his way. Odd for Nar to issue orders when I'm around. I'm sure I won't like his event report. Nar lays Mas on my bed. Puddles of blood spread over my mattress. I've never seen anything like it. The small cuts on his chest should've healed by now, but it appears they keep opening even more.

I crawl in bed next to Mas and lie on my back because that's the only way I know how to run the repair system Mas invented. I'm sure he could run it from the tower down the street while munching on snacks and talking to ten males, but that's what makes him special and invaluable to me.

"Mas, you're gonna be okay," I tell him.

Nar's pacing the room.

The repair system erects, and as soon as the laser lights up above us, I roll off the bed so it doesn't touch me. It won't kill me, but the laser burns hurt, and nobody besides me uses the system for that reason. Most males prefer to take the time to heal naturally. Luckily for Mas, he's unconscious, so he won't be screaming in my chambers.

While the repair system works on his head, assessing and fixing brain injuries first, I watch the small cuts on his chest ooze blood. I glance at Nar, who sits on my throne while I, the Kai of my people, sit at the corner of the bed like a hunter nanny. The things I endure from my brother and his sidekick on Mas's deathbed. I swear on Herea, these two will age me faster than nature intended. Therefore, it is time for a lecture.

"You stole a female from the Ra. I had to answer for that crime," I say. "Almost started a war for you. This one," I jerk my head indicating Mas, "returned from lands unknown near dead. Wanna tell me what Mas had planned, or should I torture it out of you?"

Nar lifts his palms. "I know nothing. On Herea, I swear. Mas never told me he was heading for the Blood Dunes."

"Blood Dunes!" I leap off the bed. "What the fuck was he doing there?"

"We found him lying on the sand of the Blood Dunes."

"Of all the males in the tribe, Mas would be the last one I

would call reckless." I hover over Mas. "You reckless hook-hole." There, I said it and feel lighter in my chest now.

"It makes no sense he would go there. Even for a female. It's too risky."

"I didn't think he liked womankind. He doesn't enter games, so why would he walk on the Dunes? Even the Ra don't go there."

"I don't know."

"Give me something. Any reason. Just say what you're thinking."

"Okay." Nar frowns. "Mas does what he believes is best for the tribe and the few males he cares about. He rarely does anything for himself. There are only two females in the tribe, and we marked them. Maybe he saw the error of our ways and decided to take matters into his own hands."

"You mean he decided he would secure a female for the next games, showing the tribe there's at least one male in the tribe who won't mark a female?"

"It sounds like Mas, no?"

"But?" I prompt.

"It's unlike Mas to hide his intentions from you."

I nod. "There must be another reason."

"When we got there, the female was petting his hunter."

"Petting?" I scratch my belly.

Nar shudders. "Blood was pooling all around him, and she sat there and kept petting him, spreading his blood on the rest of his body. And, awkwardly, hers." Nar touches his cheek and draws an imaginary blood line.

My turn to shudder. "As if dipping her finger in paint and marking the face, promising the male a win in the games." During the games, we paint our bodies, and the female, if she favors a male over the other, paints hers in the same pattern as her favored male. Herea, goddess of the hunt, would make the males paint their bodies with their own blood. She banned the ritual when she realized her daughter soaked up the power from the ritual. But it was too late. By the time Herea figured out bloodletting fed Eme power, Eme struck and ended Herea's reign. Since Herea was the goddess of the hunt and also harmony, the predators started warring.

The smell of rising fear penetrates my chambers. Both my brother and I fear something, though we can't quite point our fingers at it, which tells me Mas uncovered a goddess, one all in the lands fear. We don't fear what we can kill, and we can kill everything and anyone, but the goddesses are powerful, forces we try to understand, but fail to time and time again. They've returned to walk among us, test us, tempt us, fuck us, breed with us, and, if we're not careful, annihilate us.

Herea is the most popular and strongest of them all. She hates weakness. Fear is a weakness. I rein in mine. "You think the female is..." I don't speak her name. The one whose power still haunts that part of Ra territory. I don't want her in the tribe. Ark can have her.

Nar shrugs. "Mas will know."

Mas groans, looking a bit more alive now as the repair system replicates the flesh on his thigh to add the missing chunk of his flesh. A scream rips out of Mas's chest, and his hunter starts pushing against the male's skin. Nar and I wince and cover our ears. This hurts worse than an arrow in the eye. I'd know. I've suffered both. I'm happy to see Mas will recover. A tiny evil part of me is rejoicing in his scream-ing. I can't wait to find out what was possibly going through Mas's head. Wind, I presume.

CHAPTER THIRTEEN

MAS

During the Ra attack, Eme went into the tent to get my ax. She then returned when I was down and struck the Ra, probably not even aware she did it. She offered food and water and was fun to be around. Mature yet spontaneous, Eme fascinates me.

Surprised and puzzled, I want to peel back all her layers and take a peek inside her. There's something hidden in there, something the scriptures don't mention, something nobody knows beside her. While the others called her Eme the Bloodletter behind her back, during the time she reigned the lands, she asked to be addressed as Her Grace.

When I read the scriptures mentioning Eme, I always imagined her as a beautiful, graceful goddess, sitting on a throne and amusing herself with the suffering of bleeding predators. But graceful doesn't quite equate with grace. Grace is many things. Elegance, politeness, courtesy. But also benevolence, favor, and charity.

This is the Eme I met. Her Grace. My tribemates will bleed each other when they see her, but they won't compete for Eme the Bloodletter. We need a party, one where Eme will lure everyone in with her dance. In secret, however, I wish no one saw her as the goddess of grace. I want her grace all for myself. This is why I have to get those games going as soon as possible.

Fingers touch my eyelids and peel them open. Hart's face comes into view, and he's hovering, hair a bit messy at the top, meaning he's run his claws through it, probably done some pacing around the room, trying to understand why I did what I did, namely went off to the Blood Dunes without telling him about it.

"Am I fixed?" I ask.

Hart walks away, and I blink, then scrub my face, wiggle my feet, and flex my muscles. Soreness near my left hip, right flank, upper chest...actually, the entire body. Looking down, I see I'm whole, if covered in blood and sand. The mattress soaked up the blood.

Nar's sitting on Hart's throne.

Hart's over by the window, back turned toward me.

I glance over at Nar, who runs a claw over his throat, telling me Hart may wanna cut me.

"I will get you another mattress, Kai." I address him as Hart most often, but right now, Kai is best.

My Kai turns slowly. "You're worried about my mattress?"

I shake my head. This conversation will go as well as I imagined.

Nar walks to Hart's closet and gets a fluffy pillow to tuck under my head. He pets me, smiling like a hooker. Now that I've survived, he's enjoying this. He's the one usually in trouble with our Kai.

"How is the female?" I ask.

"Unconscious," Nar says.

Hart hasn't spoken yet, which tells me he's reining in his aggression. I feel it crawling under my skin, getting my hunter riled up, but I stand down, or rather keep lying there, casual and calm. I need to play this well, guide the conversation, ease into the Blood Dunes.

"What news of Gur's territory?"

"Ark's still there," Nar says. Having Ark near the capital and with hundreds of males ready at his disposal for war makes Hart more aggressive than usual. Amti is pregnant and crazier than ever, talking to herself as she walks the streets, so my Kai is feeling protective and maybe also mad.

"Ark has secured several females for our tribe," Nar says. "He says he'll deliver after he deals with Gur's territory."

"Who is fighting for Gur's earldom?" I ask.

"Lor, the subtribe that was already there, and Feli."

"After Gur, Feli should be next in line," I say. "Who is Ark standing with?"

"With whoever will support him when the time comes for him to face his opposition," Nar says. Ark's gonna shed blood for the Ra throne. It's only a matter of time.

"Even if that supporter wants to war with us?" I ask, glancing at Hart, who's watching me, saying nothing. His silence kills me on the inside. It's like he turned off the lights. He does it on purpose so I can feel what it's like when one doesn't have the support and strength of a hunter Alpha male. Makes me feel alone, like a stray puppy, and I hate the feeling.

"We need to strategically place someone there. Whichever one of them wants peace with us."

Nar nods. "Agreed. Do you know which of the three males wants peace?" Nar asks, trying to get Hart to talk.

Hart grunts. He won't be baited. He'll talk when he's good and ready. Fuck.

"I could release Feli's portal controls if he agrees to follow the peace treaty. Or better yet, we can use his controls as leverage."

"Ah, here we come at last," Hart says and sits on the bed. "I wasn't aware you hacked Feli's controls."

I scoot away from Hart. "Not just any portal controls. The game controls." Game controls often hide other portals the game master set up, which was why I cracked his. We now have new secret entries into Ra territory and even other territories. Feli wasn't as bad at portal mastery as I thought he was. He's pretty good, actually, but I'm still better.

Hart leans in inches from my face. Orange hunter eyes watch me, make my hunter stir. "Quit evading and tell me the where and why and what of the Blood Dunes." He lingers a bit longer only to get my hunter to growl at him. Smirking, Hart leans back but keeps sitting on the bed.

I prop myself up with a grunt. Fuck, I'm sore. Could use a nap. "During the Ra games, they shoved me into the Blood Dunes portal. They thought the spirit of Eme would bleed me, I believe. When I found my way back, Feli pushed me into the hole with traps that bled me almost to death, so Eme got her blood anyway."

"Funny, you said it was a dead-end portal," Hart says. "You lied to me. Why did you lie, Mas?"

"I'm sure there's a good reason he lied," Nar says. "Tell him the reason, Mas."

"On the sand, I saw the footprints. Five toes on each foot. Didn't want anyone to know I'd returned for her. I thought you'd send males with me and risk their lives or prohibit me from returning."

"You're right. I would prohibit you from returning. It is my right to do so."

"But I couldn't leave a breeder stranded there. Nobody would come for her."

Hart leans in again. "Is it Herea?" he whispers.

I shake my head.

Hart seems relieved.

"Wait, your wounds wouldn't heal," Nar says.

I watch my Kai and see the second it hits him. His eyes bug out, and he stands. "Are you mad, bringing Eme to the tribe?"

I smile. "Possibly I am."

Nar coughs. "Amti."

"Oh, so now my Amti is an excuse for Mas's lies and reckless endangerment?"

A portal opens, and Hart moves away from it. In walks Amti from the baths, head down, looking at her hands. "That was so funny." She wiggles her fingers, giggling.

Is she talking to her fingers? I believe so. This does not bode well for us. I glance at Nar as Amti closes the portal on the third try. The first try made the portal entrance shrink, and Hart's gonna have to fix it, or soon he won't have access to his baths. Do you understand now why I cannot have anyone touching my portals?

"Oh, hi," Amti says, finally looking up from her fingers. "Didn't know we had company." She smiles and tucks her curls behind her ear, her gaze finding my middle. She turns red in the face and drops her gaze to the floor.

Hart opens the closet and throws a fur over my body. Lips curling into a snarl, he says, "Return Eme to where she belongs."

Here we go. "The Ra hunters came after her. It's how I ended up injured."

"Let 'em have her. There will be no blood games in the Ka tribe."

"Wait. Hold on," Amti interrupts. "Who is Eme?"

"Nobody," Hart says, while I snag the opportunity as it presents itself. "Eme is a womankind. I delivered her the medicine and brought her here."

"I am so relieved you found her and she's well." Amti sits

at the edge of the bed, close to my foot. She pats my calf. "Good job, Mas."

Hart's gonna kill me. I scoot as far away from her as possible.

"When can I meet her?" Amti looks at Hart.

"Never. She is going back."

Ignoring what the Kai said, Amti turns to me. In the tribe, we do not ignore our Kai. Ever. If we do, we pay for it. Amti does things we can't which means... Amti does things we can't. I could use her to help Eme, and I will. "If I return her, she'll die. Ra hunters will consume her. If not the Ra, then she'll eventually go insane in isolation. If she doesn't starve. She won't survive out there." Eme would survive, I believe. I really do. That's what bothers me, I think. It's as if she doesn't need me to protect her. But I want to.

"You can't send that woman back," Amti says to Hart.

"I can."

"But you won't," Amti says.

"Eme is evil."

"So am I. So is every goddess. So are you. So is everyone. Each of us is also good. In the tribes, there's a goddess of the hunt and harmony. Fertility and war. Which is Eme?"

"Blood and grace," I say.

"And grace," Amti repeats. "Treat her well, and the enemies will get blood while we get grace."

I couldn't have said it better myself. Amti seems cute and harmless, but there's wisdom lurking behind the eyes. Plus she has the Kai's ear, cock, and soon his puppies. She'll deliver the first young in the Ka tribe since we can remember. I should pray to her more often, but for now, I await the Kai's decision.

Hart walks to the throne, and Nar gets up so the Kai can sit. He levels me with a look I'm familiar with. "Return the female." He taps the throne's armrest and ascends into the hall, leaving us all shocked down in the chambers.

Amti's staring up at the ceiling, eyes narrowed. She smiles, looking like something terribly evil.

"He'll change his mind," she says.

Nar and I lock gazes. He looks like he wants to bolt. Most goddesses' powers can be seen or witnessed. Aoa's thunder when she lashed out at Gur, for example. But Amti's madness affects the mind.

Her giggle creeps me out.

Standing, I lean on Nar, and we walk to the bath's portal. I'm fixing it for my Kai while Nar taps his foot. "Hurry up," he hisses at my ear.

She creeps him out too.

CHAPTER FOURTEEN

TATYANA

A single-bed, minimalist room feels like a prison cell. Not that I've ever been to alien prison (or a human one). The males left, locking the door behind them while I faked unconsciousness. That's what they say to do when faced with some of the predatory animals we have on Earth. Maybe bears? I can't remember. It must have worked, because I'm still alive and sitting on the bed, crusted dried blood sticking to my palms.

Back at the wall, I pull up my legs and rest my chin on my knees, staring at the door, anticipating the moment when they'll barge back in, grab me and...who knows, take me to their kitchen so the cook can make a meal out of me.

I shouldn't have believed Mas. Yearning to get back home or to any civilization got the best of me, and I didn't see the forest for the trees, so to speak. Even with predator-class aliens, if I was on Joylius, all this wouldn't be so bad. At least then I'd have hope that National Security and our warrior aliens would find me, but since Mas informed me I'm on another planet, I realize I might never see home again.

Until I saw his predatory form, I was content, even happy

he'd come to rescue me. Hell, I was even okay after I realized he was a predator and those males who came to the camp to eat me were like him. In a way, he defended his food, which is better than tearing into me right then and there.

But lying about Joylius somehow feels worse. I held on to this belief I was on a familiar planet and it was just a matter of time before I'd be found. The belief kept me alive. It never occurred to me the pod would've landed elsewhere. They're not supposed to land on random planets. That's what the preflight briefing said.

Did Mas lie again? About me not being on Joylius? God, I just don't know.

The door clicks, signaling someone's entering. I stand, looking around for anything I can throw at whoever comes through the door, and spot Mas's knife on the bed. Not only have they not taken it away from me, one of them left it on the bed next to me. They're either stupid or forgetful or toying with me. I'd bet on the latter. Mas certainly isn't stupid, despite what National Security classification says about predators. The descriptions used for this alien classification give us an illusion this class only wants to kill and eat. That they don't have other urges, or, hell, sometimes I've seen the predator class being described as animals with no speech. The fact is either National Security has no fucking clue, or they've chosen to placate the masses so nobody panics as we travel across space.

The door opens slowly, and Mas walks inside. He's healed, and his hair drapes over his chest, still wet. I grab the knife and scoot into the corner farthest away from him. My heart's beating so loudly, it's drumming in my ears, and I'm so scared, I might just pee myself.

Casually, Mas leans back against the closed door. White eyes lock with mine, and he smiles, swiping a thumb over his lips, then licking the bottom one. He worries it between his sharp teeth and nicks a place in the corner. Blood wells, and he pushes from the door and walks toward me, and I want to melt into the wall.

I stick out the knife. "Don't come closer, or I swear I'll stab you."

Mas stops as the knife touches the middle of his chest. Blood slowly drips from the cut on his lip, and he smiles, orange eyes lurking behind the white. Those are animal eyes. I remember them well. He's gonna grow massive teeth, a tail, and claws and swallow me.

A whine escapes me. My hand shakes.

Mas pushes forward, and the tip of the knife pierces his skin.

I gasp.

He doesn't. He leans in further, forcing more of the knife into him.

"What are you doing?" I whisper.

Mas grips my wrist and, leaning in to kiss me, pushes my hand down, carving a path from the middle of his chest to his navel.

I turn my cheek away and drop the knife.

He kicks it away and crowds me, his warm body like a blanket in a freezing night.

"Just get it over with," I say and angle my head to expose my neck. "Tear it out first so I don't suffer. It's the least you can do for someone you had a...an intimate relationship with, if only for one night."

Mas kisses my neck, licks a path up to my jaw, then back down. A soft purr rises in the room, and he takes my hand and puts it over his thick, hard shaft. "I'm not hungry. I'm horny. Though I won't lie, you taste delicious." He licks behind my ear and groans. "I never intended to hurt you."

I snort. "I get it. You just wanted breakfast."

"At the time, I admit I was confused, but my hunter isn't, and he would never hurt you."

The hunter must be his animal form. Jesus. Of all things for it to be, it has to be a hunter. Why couldn't it be like an owl or a squirrel? Elephant?

He continues, "Let's start over, hm?"

Men. They're the same across the universe. When they fuck up, they wanna start over, as if that would erase everything. "I just wanted some reassurance I'm no longer alone in the middle of nowhere."

"You still have that," he says, and blows on my neck. I try to move away, but he slaps his palms against the wall. "You're definitely not alone or in the middle of nowhere now. You're in Kalia, the capital of Ka tribal territory, where a thousand predators would bleed for a chance to win you. They'd kill to do what I got to do with your little pussy. Believe me, you're safer here than with your humankind, seeing as their ship malfunctioned and you could've died." He nips my neck, and my nipples perk. I'm trying not to be aroused, but he smells like…wet wild sex, blood, and something terribly masculine.

He takes my hand and slips it through the opening in his kilt. He makes us grip his shaft together and give it a tug. He kisses the side of my neck. "My wounds are healing, Eme." He drags his tongue over my collarbone, and I clamp my thighs together. "It tells me you want me."

"My name is not Eme."

"Your name is whatever I call you."

I push against his chest, then look down at the cut closing before my eyes. Oh my God. This is unbelievable. I run a finger over the long cut and look up into the eyes of a hunter animal.

Mas takes my finger and puts it in my mouth while he strokes himself. He leans in and takes the finger from my mouth and directs it over my nipple, then circles there, and my eyelids flutter as my body heats up.

"You may not like what you've heard of my people from the humans, but you like this thing between us."

"You tricked me."

He pinches my nipple.

"The only tricked one here is me, Eme. You don't even have to try to trick me. I was yours the second I saw you dance on the Blood Dunes." He grabs my throat and squeezes, as if punishing me for something. He licks across my mouth. "You taste incredible." His purr intensifies.

"You made me think you were a warrior," I say, breathless. "Had I known you were a predator, I would never have touched you."

"You're touching me now."

I freeze my hand in his hair and pull it back, but he chuckles. "Eme, you picked your favorite, and now you'll have to go through with it."

"I picked nothing."

He pushes a knee between my legs, spreading them. Fingers graze my thigh, lifting my dress. He grabs my hip firmly with one hand and touches my swollen folds with the other. I don't want him, and I do want him. I fist a hand in his hair again, and he returns the favor while stroking my pussy, sometimes dipping inside my channel to grab moisture to spread over my clit. I pant and lean my head against the wall.

Mas pecks my lips. "Open and taste me." He pushes his tongue inside my mouth and swirls it there, and I grip his hair with both hands, feeling the coarse, inhuman strands threading through my fingers.

Mas practically eats my mouth. I've never been kissed like this before. He said he wasn't hungry, but it sure feels like he wants to devour me. He purrs so loudly, it's almost growling, and his breathing is frantic like mine, which makes me feel like he wants me. I know passion when I encounter it. It burns through a person and shines outward, and I can feel it.

I don't want this madness and lust, and yet, I want to fuck this predator. His touch ignites my body, makes me want to do everything dirty and forbidden. I want to break out into a dance nobody choreographed. Let him touch me in places I've never been touched. Inside, in the heart, where the passion burns like wild fire. But first, I want to shock myself. I want to break the rules.

Don't eat that burger, Tatyana.

Can't wear heels tonight, Tatyana. The feet need rest.

Practice starts at four, not at seven like everyone else. You are not everyone else.

Your toe is broken? Your big toenail peeled off? Too bad. Quit whining, Tatyana. That's what it takes to be a prima.

Making out with Mas means I ate the burger, wore the heels, and ruined my feet in heels. I rise to the tips of my toes and throw a leg over his hip, locking him to me. Mas removes his fingers from my pussy and detaches from my lips. Orange animal eyes stare back at me.

I am so scared of those eyes. Yet, I'm so turned on by his inhumanity that it makes me feel both guilty, rebellious, and uninhibited at the same time.

I'm flirting with death. He could snap me in half at any moment, and yet he won't, or maybe he will and this is foreplay. But I have nothing left to lose but to lose myself in this predator.

He reaches between us and puts his wide tip on my wet entrance, teasing my pussy, not pushing inside. I moan as he moves his cock and puts it at my back hole, where he rubs the moisture accumulated on his cock. He goes back and forth between my pussy entrance and my small hole, spreading my wetness below.

"I can't decide which hole I want to fuck first," Mas says.

He takes my arms and throws them over his shoulders. Sharp teeth nip my earlobe. I hiss as the skin breaks and rake my nails down his neck. Mas purrs loudly, the cock at my entrance pulsing, spurting liquid all over my pussy and ass. He reaches between us and scoops up some of his semen and puts it on his lips. He licks it as if it's honey, and then sticks his tongue into my mouth.

He tastes sweet and spicy and unexpected, and I moan.

Mas rears back. "Yummy?"

Heat crawls up my cheeks. I can't remember the last guy who could make me blush, but this one sure has more than once.

Mas puts me down and pushes at my shoulders. He puts his cock at my lips, where cum spurts on them. I lick more, and he groans, growling at the same time. I splay my hand over his abdomen, feeling those fantastic muscles shift under my touch. This predator is built like a god. I sneak my hand behind him and grab his ass, squeeze.

Mas taps his cock on my lips and pushes a thumb into my mouth, pressing down on my lower jaw, forcing it open. He fits himself inside my mouth. Grabbing my hair with both hands, he starts moving my head while I hold on to his ass cheeks and feel them moving as he pumps his cock inside my mouth, more often than not hitting the back of my throat. I gag, tears staining my face. He watches me, no longer purring but growling loudly, his eyes pools of orange, both alarming and sexy.

As he hisses, his ass gets rock hard, his abdominal muscles tighten, and he gushes his seed into my mouth. There's so much of it that I choke as it streams down my throat while Mas's body trembles with release. I grab the back of his hard thighs and hold on to them, digging my nails into his skin. Something bloodthirsty awakens inside me, and I wish I had claws I could rake down his skin and bleed him. I want to hate him.

I don't hate him.

Mas's tremors subside, and he looks down at me, then swipes a thumb over the corner of my lip and tastes his seed. I'd never seen a man do this. Not even in porn. There's something so sexy about a male who has no shits to give about perceptions or rules or anything. He does what he wants whenever he wants and however he likes it done. His confidence is alluring.

Mas crouches in front of me, and I lean in to kiss him, then rise back up and spread my legs and lift my dress. He kneels and kisses my folds, making out with those lips the same way he kisses me, twirling his tongue, flicking my clit, one palm splayed over my belly, thumb pulling up my mound for better access. I rest my heel on his shoulder and let the predator eat me.

CHAPTER FIFTEEN

MAS

We sit in comfortable silence on my small bed, me leaning against the wall, her head in my lap. I draw circles with my claw over her shoulder. It's strange for me. I share comfortable silence with only one other person, Nar, and nobody else, not even my brother.

"Nothing will happen to you," I say. "You are Eme."

"Okay, I'll bite. Who is Eme?"

"Eme is the goddess of blood and grace, the daughter of Herea..." I pause when someone knocks on the door. "Get lost," I bark.

"Mas, my boy," the Sha-male whispers. "I cannot stand the wait any longer."

"Good." I press the room controls. "Here's our Sha. He'll tell you all you want to know about Eme."

The door slides open. The Sha-male stands there, face painted in his blood from the cut across his forehead. Blood drips down into his eyes, nose, mouth, beard, and onto his wrinkled body. He wears a white cloth over his middle and carries his shaft. It takes me a moment to realize he's prepared himself as a sacrifice for Eme.

"Good Lord." Eme sits up, naturally alarmed. Even I'm fucking alarmed. Never have I seen such a thing in my life. Heard of it? Sure. But not seen it, and Hart won't like this. He ordered me to return Eme for this very reason. Before we know it, all the males will start cutting themselves or, worse, offering what the Sha is about to offer.

The Sha-male wavers on his feet. "Accept my sacrifice and spare the young males," he says. He presses a claw to his throat and tilts his head back.

"Nooooo!" Eme screams.

The Sha stops, bunching his eyebrows together. "No?"

"No. Jesus." She's up and shaking, raking hands though her hair. "What the hell is wrong with everyone here?"

"We are all mad," the Sha-male explains as if that's helpful. "Amti will give us young."

With a groan, I stand and examine his cuts. He's cut major blood vessels on his forehead and the temples. If I don't get him help, I doubt he'll heal around Eme. He's gonna bleed like a terrik.

Before he passes out in the hallway, I help him to my bed and lay him down. I pull up the portal controls and call Hart, then wait, knowing he won't answer. He's mad at me. I try him several times, and he blocks my access. I can force an entry into his chambers and push the Sha in there, but Hart might really kill me for that.

"I'll return," I tell the stunned Eme, then grab the Sha and walk into the tower control center. The males monitoring the portals across the lands stop and stare.

"Call the Kai. Tell him the Sha-male is gonna die on us if he doesn't get under the repair system."

"He'll heal," a male says.

"No, he won't," I counter.

My brother Tis comes forward and takes the Sha from me. "Why not, brother?"

Here we go. "Because you and Nar brought back Eme from the Blood Dunes."

Years ago, when we were boys, Tis and I were setting up traps. I don't know what he did, but the sharp metal trap closed over his cock. I remember the look on his face when he realized his cock got clamped. The look on his face right before he wailed in pain. He was eight. I was eleven. His cock recovered, no big deal, but his shocked expression stayed with me. I'm seeing it now, the blank shocked face with wide eyes. I see the moment he's processed what I said.

"I'll get Nar, and we'll put her back," he says.

"No can do. Eme stays. Games're opening as soon as I'm ready."

Nobody cheers. "What?" I bark. "Nobody wants to compete for Eme?" I'm offended. They have no idea what they're missing out on. Eme is bloody amazing. "You idiots. Get out of my way." I initiate a portal link to Hart's chambers, and he opens because it's from a control center, not my room.

I rush to tell him it's about the Sha before he cuts me off.

Hart moves through the portal and appears inside the tower. He grabs the Sha. Before returning to his chambers, he turns. "I cannot have males bleeding on my streets. Return Eme. Destroy the Blood Dunes portal." Hart walks away.

Fuck. Where is Amti? Is she not gonna change Hart's mind? Come on, Amti. By Herea's fine tits, I shouldn't need to rely on crazy Amti for Eme's well-being.

"You sure it's Eme and not…you know, the other one."

"Herea?" I say.

The males grumble. We love Herea, but we don't wanna call her on purpose. Praying to her, cursing her, cursing with her name stamped on it is one thing, but with goddesses walking the lands, we don't want her in the tribe. Ark can have her.

"Yes, I'm sure."

Tis nods and rubs the back of his neck. "Games, you say?" There's a glint in his eyes. I don't think he wants to win Eme, but Tis loves the games. He's only played for Amti before, and once you get a taste of the games, you want more of them.

"I'll have them up and running soon." Something presses against my lungs, and I rub my chest. I'm feeling all kinds of awkward lately.

"Brother, Hart or Nar can handle the portals for the games."

"I run the portals, Tis. There will be no touching my portals during the games. It's complicated, and I'm... I've waited all my life for the games, and I only got to master one."

"Mas, don't be stupid. She petted your hunter."

"Herea's holy tits," Dek says. "You're favored. If you don't compete, the goddess will take offense. You're fucking competing, Mas."

"I'm the portal master. Competing is out of the question."

As one, the males step back and stare at the doorway of the control center.

I turn to see Eme. She holds my dagger in her hand. "Mas, I'm looking for a bathroom." She swallows. Her fear makes my gums swell. Next to me, my brother purrs, and before I can think, I snap my teeth at his cheek, nicking his skin.

Tis wipes the blood, licks it. "You sure you won't compete?"

Chuckles sound in the room.

"Get back to work," I grumble, then stomp out, laughter ringing behind me.

CHAPTER SIXTEEN

TATYANA

I expect the bathroom to be in the room. When I can't find it, I think maybe they have shared bathrooms since this building isn't a single home. As I find the door unlocked, I creep down the dimly lit hallway lined with sliding doors until I reach what I'd call a lobby, a circular room with five wide openings at the walls leading to rooms filled with males in kilts, who sensed or smelled me the second I stepped into the lobby.

Faced with so many predators, I feel as if time stopped, and I whimper. My bladder threatens to empty right then and there, but then I hear Mas's voice and scurry toward him. Inside one of the rooms, he's speaking with a male who looks just like him, but with golden-blond hair pulled up into a messy ponytail. It's the same male from the beach. They exchange unpleasantries, and Mas seems upset as he stomps out of the room and into the lobby, stopping at the center of it.

"Are you coming?" he bites out.

I don't care for his bad mood, and I snort as I approach him. "You're having a bad day, huh?"

"One could say that." Mas grabs my shoulders, and the ground under us starts to turn. I stare at the circular shape as it descends into the floor and starts spinning faster. Wha... The circle drops like a freefall roller coaster at the amusement park. A scream rips out of me, and I plaster my body to his and dig my fingernails into his back, holding on for dear life.

Just before the spinning stops and we hit the ground, Mas lifts me. We land with a thud, and I'm fairly certain that if he hadn't lifted me, the impact would've reverberated in my spine and rattled my brain.

Mas steps off, still carrying me, a smile playing on his lips. "I'm not in a bad mood anymore." He bends his head, clearly intent on kissing me as he walks outside, passing a predator who is on the way in. I keep pulling back, away from Mas's lips, but he's following with his mouth, and when I have nowhere to go, I bend my back all the way so my head ends up between his calves. Mas stops.

I grip his ankle and execute a simple backflip. Standing, I wipe a hand on my thigh. "Bathroom."

He's on me in a second, mouth on mine, holding my hip and my head so I can't wiggle away. I throw up my hands and kiss him back. There's no escaping this guy. He takes what he wants when he wants it, and, if I'm being honest, the fact he can't seem to resist touching or kissing me bodes well for my ego, not to mention my libido.

When I'm preparing for a big show, like the solo performance on Joylius, I live and breathe ballet, sometimes for a year or more. This means I eat, sleep, dance. Nothing else. I attend no side gigs, I see no friends, I have no days off. Pulling off a memorable performance worthy of millions of televiews in addition to thousands of people in the arena requires perfection, and perfection can only be attained by hard work and razor-sharp focus.

Since my midthirties, when I realized I was at the tail end of my career, I've performed several thousand shows, some harder on me than the others. Not to mention age does a body no good, and I'm not as agile as I used to be. All this is to say I've not had an intimate relationship since my early thirties, and before that, I dated the senator who almost killed me.

I survived him.

I've broken my toes countless times and danced on, bleeding.

I've starved myself most of my life too. I've had bad things happen to me, and yet, I'm still around. Therefore, I can survive this predator problem I have right now. Males *booo* as they pass us, and Mas chuckles. He jerks his head. "This way."

We walk down a street lined with huts and predator Vikings in space. The lack of women makes me uneasy, and I recall our conversation about the hunter earlier when I didn't know what Mas was actually talking about. "When you talked about the hunter and no females, you meant there're no females in…in your…tribe?"

Mas nods, eyes on the massive door of the imposing massive obsidian tower as we cross the bridge. The river below it races with the current. Turning, I see males following us. Lots of males. And more joining, all with white eyes, but some also flashing orange. I pick up the pace.

"They can smell your fear," Mas says and walks faster with me. I glance back at the same time as one of the males drops to all fours, bones pushing and prodding under his skin. I freeze and can't look away as his body makes a transition into his hunter form. He rears back, orange eyes glowing, teeth exposed, and releases a bloodcurdling cry.

Liquid tickles down my thighs.

The male in hunter form snaps his mouth shut. The males climbing the bridge after us all stop dead in their tracks. Mas starts laughing his head off, bending over the bridge railing, and I'm so embarrassed, I feel heat flush my face, neck, and chest. I cannot believe I peed myself in front of all these people, but what hurts most is that the only one who seemed to give a shit about me, and the one whose dick I just sucked, is laughing about it.

Spinning on my heel, I head toward the door and bump into a hard wall. I bounce off and rub my forehead. A massive male with dark hair and glowing orange eyes stands before me. Not a wall. I bumped his chest. He stares at the wetness on the bridge, then looks up at me, a strand of black hair falling over his face. A clawed hand extends, and I whimper, frozen in place.

Mas slaps the male's hand away.

The male lifts his upper lip, and when I think he's gonna bite Mas and me, he smiles, though it presents as a show of flesh-tearing teeth. "You must be Eme."

Silence falls in the city. Only the air traffic buzzes.

The male looks beyond me, and I turn. The one in hunter form changes back into his humanoid form, looking anywhere besides at us. He melts back into the crowd.

"Everyone," the Wall says, "meet Eme."

Everyone, as one, takes a collective step back. Chanting begins, and some males start backpedaling away.

Relieved the males have backed off, I sigh. "Thank you, sir." He's a leader of these people. I can tell. If not from the size of him, then from the air around him, and how he spoke to all when he introduced me.

"Hart," he says and extends a hand.

I shake it. He's pleasant, if scary, also kind of sexy in a broody sort of way. I'd have to be blind not to notice the collective maleness in the city. Their muscular structure is exceptional.

He turns up his palm. "Mas," he says. "You gave Eme your knife?"

"Nar left it there for her before he brought me in for repairs."

"Ah, my annoying brother. Some spans, I wanna kill him. Recently, I'm having thoughts of killing him and you quite often. Eme," he purrs. "Bad, bad girl, Eme." He shakes his head and parts his kilt, takes out his dick, and pisses right over the place I wetted.

Oh. My. God. Two things. One. A man just took out a massive cock and pissed right in front of me. Two. Said man has no extra parts at the tip of his penis.

Hart tucks himself back into his kilt and speaks as if nothing unusual has transpired. "Seeing as I have dealt with goddesses marking my territory before, I will forgive the trespass."

"Sir, I wasn't marking your—"

He lifts a palm. "Shhhh."

I snap my mouth shut. Forget pleasant. What a dick.

"Do not ever mark my territory again."

He lingers, so I say the only thing that's left to say. "Yes, sir."

He turns to Mas. "The female needs to bathe. Take very special care guarding our bad Eme, Mas. After she bathes, you know what to do. I haven't changed my mind. Understood?"

"She will use your baths, Hart," Mas says.

Hart grabs the back of Mas's neck, yanks him forward, and their chests clash. Mas starts growling, a terrible gurgling sound.

"Are you telling me or asking to use my baths?" Hart says.

"Asking, Kai."

Hart's starting to growl back, working his thumb over the pulse on Mas's neck. Hart's head moves as if he's rubbing his cheek on Mas's cheek, and Mas closes his eyes and exhales a breath.

"Forgive me, Kai."

Hart continues running a thumb over Mas's pulse. I don't know if he wants to cut him or if he's petting him. It's… It's animalistic, intimate, inhumane, and…sexy. My nipples perk up, and a rush of arousal coats my pussy lips. "Cut," I whisper.

Hart nicks him, and blood wells as the Kai steps back, eyes on me.

They can smell my arousal, and I'm mortified this is arousing to me. I'm some kind of a freak. Holly crap.

Hart licks his finger. "There you go, Eme. But know this: I will kill you before I let you bleed any of my males, especially Mas. You will get your sacrifice, but you will not kill. This is my land, and the Ka have bled enough already."

"I'm not gonna bleed anyone."

"I know. I threatened your existence. You may enjoy my private baths. I have a bathroom, soup in a bowl, flower trees, and…other feminine things."

He's pleasant again. This guy's fucking with my head too.

"Thank you."

"Anytime. Mas will show you the way."

"I don't have access to that portal," Mas say.

Hart snorts. "Sell that crap over in Ralna's market."

The male I think is Mas's brother comes running up the bridge. "What did I miss?" He looks from Mas to Hart, then sniffs, gaze dropping to the ground, then back up at Hart. He scratches his head.

"On second thought," Hart says. "Tis will show you to the baths."

Tis smiles from ear to ear, showing his sharp teeth. "Yes, Alpha."

He throws a hand over my shoulder. Mas steps near us

and slaps Tis upside his head.

Tis slaps him back while Hart's smiling. "What's the matter, Mas?"

"I'll bathe her." Mas frowns. "No, what I meant to say was I'll show her to the baths."

"Hooker," Hart says.

"I am no hooker, Kai. There will be games."

Harts snorts again. "Not in the Ka tribe. Get that out of your stubborn head. You know what to do." He winks at me. "Have a nice temporary stay."

"Temporary" doesn't escape my notice, but I smile and say, "Thank you."

"Are you done now, Kai?" Mas asks, clearly annoyed.

Hart winks and starts walking away backward. "We will still honor you, Eme. A party in your name," he shouts.

Cheers break out at the end of the bridge.

Hart continues. "This evening." He turns and gets lost in the crowd of males, who're slapping him on his back, head, ass. One even kicks him.

I turn to Mas, looking for an explanation to…all the things.

Tis lingers. "Hooker." He points a finger at Mas's chest. "At least let me kick your ass in the games."

"I run the portals in the games."

"I know," Tis says. "Because you're a hooker."

"I'm not a hooker!"

Tis smiles. "Amti's madness is spreading. Soon, we're all gonna be hookers. Three spans. Two nights. One hooker. Let the hooking begin." He laughs as he walks away.

Mas wiggles his nose. "Let's get you cleaned up."

"What happened here?"

"I'll explain later." Mas leads me inside a place that reminds me of a cathedral. Ceiling as far as the eye can see, large windows with incredible mosaic-type art on the right, and on the left, golden lines as if they're scriptures of some sort. At first, they appear as hieroglyphics to me, until letters form in my head, and the translator kicks in. In some places, golden lines pulse on the walls as if inviting me to read them.

Next to me, Mas stops.

I walk up to the wall. "Your translators are more advanced than ours, you know."

"How so?" Mas asks.

"Ours can't translate another alphabet."

"Eme," he says, voice low and weary sounding, "ours can't either."

"Sure they can." I point at the pulsing golden lines that form letters and words. "And so the daughters of Herea united to defeat their mother, thus initiating a reign of war and games." I turn to Mas. "No?"

Mas's fist is clenched and at his mouth. He looks uncertain, even freaked out, eyes roaming all over the wall.

I watch the golden lines brighten in some areas more than others, and I read where my eyes take me. There's paragraphs about Herea, Eme's mother, and a mention of the Blood Dunes, apparently the land where I crashed that I initially believed to be an uninhabited tropical paradise on Joylius. Eme sounds…terrible, demanding blood sacrifices whenever she pleased. The more blood the predators shed in wars or games, the more powerful she became. Her sister, Lyu, goddess of the games, together with Eme, demanded that predators enter the games for the right to breed both females and at the same time and kill each other for the honor. The games became deadly, and turn after turn, over the centuries, predator numbers dwindled while the goddesses thrived.

I stop reading. "I am not this Eme girl," I say.

"You are."

"You made a mistake. All of you did."

"I don't make mistakes."

"I don't like her."

"Not many do."

I swallow a lump in my throat. "I've never been a mean person, and I don't like to be called Eme. There's history about this woman that doesn't sit well with me."

Mas stands before a throne. He rubs his hands together and stares at the space for a few beats before wiggling his fingers and moving them over the air the same way he did in the tent.

"Are you opening a portal?" I ask.

"No. We'll take the throne down."

"That explains everything." Not. I step next to him, then fold myself onto the throne, which could fit five of me and Mas comfortably. I tap the armrest. Mas spins around at the same time as I drop below, screaming my lungs out. The second the throne stops, I jump off it, cross my legs, and bend over so I don't pee again from the rattling in my bladder and stomach. "What the hell was that?" I look up.

The throne lifts briefly, then comes back down, delivering Mas. He takes my hand. "Please don't touch anything. It seems Hart's made changes recently. For Amti, I'm sure." We pass a massive bloodstained bed, and I spot blue flip-flops at the foot of it. Are those mine? If they're not mine... "Is there another woman living here?"

"Mmhm. Amti."

I doubt that's her name, but okay. I'm going with this. I am. I have to. "She is Hart's wife?"

Mas nods and opens a portal, and I peer inside the space. There's a narrow path lined with green grass, trees, and flowers. We step through the portal and onto the path. On my left is a tent. Mas points. "The bathroom."

After finally doing my business in their version of a bathroom, I walk out of the tent. Mas isn't there, so I continue on the path and come to a lake with a waterfall and flowers and steaming hot water. On my right, I spot towels on one of the logs surrounding a low-rise table that's under a structure being built. It's a sitting area with a firepit. When I'm sure nobody's around, I undress and dip my toe in the water.

Something grabs me from behind.

I yelp and struggle when he presses me against his warm body and leaps across the entire lake, landing firmly on the rocks before the waterfall. I place my hands over my heart. "You have to stop cornering me and creeping up on me."

"I don't know what else to do with you, prey," Mas whispers, then plants a kiss under my ear and walks us under the waterfall. It's warm, a bit too warm, and I hiss as water pounds me. Minutes later, my body acclimates, and I lean the back of my head on Mas's shoulder, reaching behind me to grab his cock. I give him a few strokes, and he purrs, low and seductive, at my ear.

A hand sneaks between my legs, and his kneecaps hit the back of my knees, taking us down. We kneel facing the rock as Mas holds me by my throat, his agile fingers working my pussy, pumping it fast. I spread my legs wider, and he slaps my entrance.

I yelp and close my legs.

He bends forward and takes my body with him so that my breasts rest over my thighs. Mas runs a palm down my back and captures both my wrists. His grip is firm as he presses them to the small of my back. He positions his cock in my hands and moves it over them. I grab him as best as I can from this position. His cock, smooth and hard, travels between my ass cheeks and over my palms, back and forth this way, teasing me, making me frustrated he won't just fuck me.

Fingers graze my entrance, and I moan as he strokes my lips, then my small back hole. I relax and close my eyes, completely surrendering to him in the same way I surrender to music, sometimes letting it take me to highs that don't exist on a conscious plane.

Mas folds himself over me and nips my ear, kisses my cheek. "Not many like Eme. They fear her. Eme was independent, and that kind of independence can drive a male mad. Eme took care of herself. She didn't need males to do anything for her. Like Herea, Eme hunted predators. Grown males she bedded, then disposed of, going on her merry way. It's alluring. A female one can never have for one's own."

Mas probes my small hole with his thumb, and I relax my muscles even more. "That-a girl," he praises me. "But the scriptures don't reveal everything about her." Mas pushes another finger inside my pucker hole and spreads them, stretching me, prepping me, and I moan. "Nobody ever saw her dance. Not the way I have. They also never saw her smile or be kind to a predator, offer him food, water, and lots of loving." He removes his fingers, and the hard tip of him grazes my hole. He circles it, and the thing at the top of his cock hardens more before he pushes his cock inside me, breaching me.

"I think"—Mas slaps his palms on the ground on either side of me, trapping me—"Eme just needs a reminder of who's a predator and who's not." Slowly, he moves inside me, and his cock stretches my ass until the wide top enters and then Mas stops and withdraws, then pushes inside, this time deeper. I sneak a hand between my legs and rub my clit, sometimes dipping my fingers inside my pussy.

He spreads my ass cheeks and fucks me, and I pant louder and louder until I find my release. The orgasm is forceful and lasts for a full minute, small tremors continuously running through my body while my face is resting on the warm ground. My eyes close, and I'm completely sated. I sigh. "You're mine, hunter," I say.

CHAPTER SEVENTEEN

MAS

L eaning back, I exhale as my cock pumps seed inside her secret hole, the one that must be satisfied for a goddess to remain happy with whatever male she's chosen to lure into her trap.

"You're mine, hunter," Eme whispers in a language so old, even I can barely make out the words.

The hair on my arms stands on end, and a shiver runs down my spine. Knowing she's Eme and hearing the language of the old from a female who couldn't possibly have learned it or ever heard of it creeps me out.

I rub her back and withdraw from her, gather her up, and hold her for a bit. Although Eme the goddess is fierce, the womankind is gentle and kind. I kiss her cheek, and we sit while I listen to her breathing.

"Toward the end of Eme's reign, she became a recluse," I start. "Scriptures in the Ra tribe say Eme sought a companion, and the males who won the games didn't quite measure up. Scriptures over in the Om tribe say Eme visited Mount Omila once in search for the male who would dare mark her. Of course, nobody would."

"Mark her how?"

"Release the hook."

"Ah, the thing at the tip of your cock. And what happens when it's released?"

"The female can only be bred by that one male. We don't do that anymore. Well, we didn't. Shouldn't. Can't."

"Why not?"

"We are near extinction, and every female counts. Besides, females move from male to male with freedom. It is our way."

Eme hums. I believe she likes hearing this. Of course she likes it. The Ra and Om tribes don't know what they're talking about.

"What do the Ka scriptures say?" she asks.

"We believe Eme was a ruthless goddess who started the Ka males' path of extinction by demanding that predators sacrifice themselves during wars or games."

She chuckles. "No wonder your guys came after me on the street."

"Your scent confuses them, that's all. But with time, as we get used to womankind living among us, we will be able to scent the difference between you all individually and as a species. Since you're both a breeder and prey, it's an experience we haven't encountered in nature before."

"A breeder," she says in a way that doesn't ask a question, but I go on to explain anyway because Eme is the maker of her faith, and I believe she couldn't have picked a better womankind for what she needs. A tough, mature woman who lets loose with her passions and experiences them. I just love her.

Swallowing, I continue. "We are trying to survive as a tribe much in the same way you survived the crash. If you think womankind crashing all over our lands is something we encounter often, you'd be wrong. We're all adjusting as time passes. Learning. Growing in mind and body."

Eme shifts in my arms and looks up.

When I don't meet her gaze, she yanks my beard.

I look down and lose myself in her sea-colored eyes.

"You're pretty deep, Mas."

"Someone has to be." I lift my nose, sniffing out Nar. "Here comes my other half. The winded one." I wink and stand, hands on my hips.

Eme folds her legs and arms in a way that covers her body.

"Why are you here when you know Eme is bathing?" I ask.

Nar covers his eyes and dangles a piece of cloth between his claws. "Aoa sent clothes."

"Thank you very much." Eme shouts as if he can't hear her from afar. "Who's Aoa?" she asks me.

"You'll meet her at the party tonight." Walking a few steps toward the edge of the rock, I bend at the knees and tap around, searching for nonslippery ground. Jumping from solid ground and jumping from a wet rock aren't the same thing, which makes the leap difficult. But I intend to impress Eme with my fitness since I won't get to compete for her, and she'll never know how fit I am.

I leap off and immediately know I'm not gonna make it. I hit the water with a massive splash, sink to the bottom, then bounce back out to land next to Nar, who peeks between his fingers. "Keep practicing," he says.

I snatch the clothes from him and hop over to the logs, where I find her a towel. Just as I prepare to return for her, she bounces off the rock and dives headfirst into the baths. Eme showing me her fitness makes my chest expand. I'm unsure what is happening to my chest lately. Around her, it seems to inflate and deflate. A strange biological response. I'll think on it later.

I drop the clothes on the table. Nar lands next to me, sits down, and pats the log. He wants to chat? Why now? I have a naked female in the private baths. Emphasis on private. "Can we chat some other time? I'm a little busy now."

"I was busy with Aoa, but that didn't stop you from chatting with me. Sit your ass down."

I shake off the water, squeeze it out of my beard, and run fingers through my hair. I enjoy baths, but hate being wet at the same time. My back's to Eme. Without a word, we switch places so his back is to her.

Sometimes I feel like he's inside my head. Lots of times, we don't have to talk to understand each other. What I wouldn't give to have something similar with a female.

Nar leans his elbows on his knees. "We must have games."

I nod. "And we will."

"Hart's not gonna hold them."

I shake my head. "Eme must have games."

"And you?"

"What about me?"

"How do you feel about holding games for Eme?"

I frown at the deflation in my chest. "I don't know anything about feelings, but there will be games as soon as I get the terrain ready. Currently, I'm thinking about the terrain I want to set up."

"You will guard Eme during the games, then."

"Naturally."

He scrubs his jaw.

I continue. "I'm the portal master. Why are you being weird?"

Nar leans in and knocks on my head. "Winded," he says.

"Not at all. I'm deep." Eme said so.

"Mas, we've warred since we were kids. Aoa said we have

wounds and other feelings and we still think the Ra are after us, and we'll probably never stop feeling like the Ra will surge on Kalia right now and we'll leave again. Our survival mode is strong. But sometimes we have to do the uncalculated stuff. For ourselves. To…to heal the feelings. Sometimes we have to follow the feels and not calculate. You're the most calculating male I know."

"We survived *because* I calculate. Our portals are the best and most guarded in all the lands."

"I know. I know, and the tribe knows. But, Mas, has it never occurred to you not to be the portal master during the games?"

I glance away. "Once. Recently. But I can't compete. Not for Eme."

Nar sighs. "Why not, Mas?"

I watch her swimming and shrug.

"Answer me," Nar pushes, and I scent aggression.

"I don't answer to you."

Nar's fist flies into my face. Blood gushes out of my nose, and I pinch the bridge of it, breathing through my mouth.

"You don't trust me?" he hisses and hits his chest. "Really, Mas? This is what it's come to?"

Fuck. I wipe my face with the cloth. "You're being dramatic."

"I'm not. You're holding back on me. It's hurting my fucking feelings."

"You don't have feelings, Nar."

"I have them. I feel for you hard, my friend." He hits his chest. "In here."

He's making sense of my chest pains. "If I compete, I'm gonna win," I say.

"Naturally."

"Naturally."

"What's the problem?" he asks.

I release the bridge of my nose. "If I win…" I swallow the rest. Shame overwhelms me.

"Tell me, or I'll never speak to you again. On Bera's fertile womb, I swear it."

"If I win, I'm gonna mark her." I pinch my lips, lock eyes with his, and feel the pressure leave my chest. I am…light-hearted at the moment. "It feels good to share that."

"Go on, Mas."

"Bera delivered Eme with her own two hands out of Herea's womb and blessed her with birthing girls. Females, Nar. You understand what this means?"

"Blessed Eme. We ought to pray to her more often."

"Eh, not quite."

"Continue. I'm curious about how you're reasoning out of marking her."

"Eme should bear girls again. For us, the Ka. Marked females aren't as fertile as unmarked ones. It is why the hook isn't used anymore. And Eme should remain unmarked and free and as cared for and as fertile as she can be. We should sacrifice for her."

"Hart won't allow one of us to be her sacrifice. He won't."

"I know. So she must have blood games. A party in her honor won't do." Though I presume Eme will enjoy it.

Nar stands. "You are a bigger male than I am."

Because I can't selfishly mark Eme. I won't do it. "And bigger than Hart in that sense."

Nar snickers. "But you're making a mistake."

"I don't make mistakes."

"Everyone makes mistakes."

I roll my eyes. "Since when did you become so…deep?"

"Since I hooked and you didn't. And by the way," he says, swaggering away, "your bleeding stopped. Eme favors you."

CHAPTER EIGHTEEN

TATYANA

"I take it my pod is around here somewhere?" I put on one of the dresses I would have worn after the show on Joylius for mingling with the rich and famous, who are mostly living on Mars nowadays and spending lavish seasons on Joylius. Mars has become a status symbol, and Joylius is following right behind. The wealthy spend millions traveling back and forth and staying in Joylian resorts for months at a time just so other Martians can see how they live. Inwardly, I tsk. I dislike thinking about Mars/Earth politics.

"We recovered your pod, and it's here attached to the tower," Mas replies.

"Did you find any shoes?" I ask. In the store, when I bought the simple short beige dress, I paired it with beige sandals with a cute lacy bow at the toes.

"I haven't."

I spin around the room, wishing for a mirror. There's isn't one, so I walk up to the nude Mas standing in front of a spatial opening to a closet. Mas's spinning the racks. They appear out of nowhere. The tech on this planet is pretty fantastic, as is Mas's ass. I spank it.

Mas doesn't yelp or jump or even startle. I'd hoped to get some sort of reaction out of him, but nothing. I squeeze one hard globe, and he turns his profile to me, grabbing the rack with both hands. "Okay, Eme, I'm curious what it is you want to do now."

I spank his ass again.

His jaw tightens, teeth grinding as if he's chewing his words. I press my front to his back and reach around him, then take him into my hand. Mas is hard. Mas is always hard, always ready for me, and he makes me feel like an eighteen-year-old freshman first discovering sex with a hot older frat boy and then fucking him nonstop, milking every last drop of sperm out of him.

Mas and I fucked like bunnies today. Every waking hour, we were fucking. Except Mas isn't a bunny. Mas is that pretty golden lion lounging on the grass, watching the prey graze before him and doing nothing to chase them because he knows if he watches long enough, the prey will become accustomed to his proximity, even begin to enjoy his watchful eyes.

That's what Mas has done with me.

First, he watched me. Then he approached me, gently so I would accept him, humanize him. And he kept humanizing himself until I acclimated and forgot he's a different species, not to mention a predator.

I stroke him and reach the hook, twisting that part of him. Growling, he watches me over his shoulder, hunter eyes flashing. "We should get going." He grabs a red kilt from the rack, snaps it around his waist, and turns. He wrinkles his nose. "I don't know why you have to look so pretty. Don't you have something else to wear?"

I smile. "Thank you. I could go naked."

He heads for the door, and I catch up to him. We walk a few more steps back to the lobby and stand on the circle.

Mas lifts me again. His eyes keep flashing back to his hunter form tonight, and while I'm okay with his animal form, I'm also apprehensive. After the baths and I think his secret conversation with Nar, Mas's hunter feels restless to me.

"You seem on edge," I say. We hit the ground floor and exit the tower into the street.

Mas doesn't comment, and when we get to the cathedral, at the door, he says. "Greet the other womankind and be quick about it. I don't want to stay too long."

The hall is jam-packed with males wearing all manner of short kilts and jewelry. Several males blow into various long wooden instruments, and at least three drummers with weird-looking drums made of a tablet of some sort sit around a massive bonfire in the center of the place. The music, oh, the music reminds me of pop Spanish crossed with traditional Arabic songs. Delighted, I squeal.

"It is prayer time before the dance," Mas says.

"This is how you pray?"

Mas nods, still looking irritated.

"I'm attending mass every day, then. Oh, mass and Mas."

Males start noticing us, and Mas growls low in his chest. He nudges me toward a woman with black hair, and she turns. My smile drops as I take in her white eyes, but she smiles plenty, and I quickly correct myself, plastering on my performer smile, the one I put on at the end of the show, even when during the performance my big toenail split down the middle and the nail was pinching my flesh.

"Hi," the woman says and hugs me, holding me longer than I expected, and I sigh at the familiar human touch. Her hair smells amazing, and I sniff. Wow. I want some of that.

She steps back. "I'm Michelle." She tilts her head. "You look familiar."

"Tatyana."

"Hmm, have we met before?"

"I don't think so." Though we could've at events. I'm staring at her white eyes, and I hope she doesn't notice because it's hard not to. She is human, yet one of them, and she looks...happy.

Her hands fold over her mouth. "Oh my God, I know. Stephanie!" she shouts across the room, and the males turn, some wincing, others covering their ears. Next to me, Mas appears even more irate.

"Do you have to draw attention?" he asks.

"She does." Nar throws a hand over her shoulders, giving Mas a dirty look. "What crawled up your nose?" he asks Mas.

"Nothing."

"Mmhm."

Stephanie likely didn't hear Michelle, because Michelle claps several times, bouncing on her feet. "Tatyana Walsh. Superbowl prima. I had tickets to your show in Joylius. I went to all your performances every time you were in Washington."

"Oh. How sweet. Thank you very much." Finding fans in the strangest of places.

She beams. "I'm sorry, I'll try not to freak out."

I laugh. "You can freak out anytime." Fans are the best.

The band starts jamming and most males either nod their heads or form a circle around the fire. I watch. The dance is something primal and old, like a haka performed on game day. The males move in a circle formation around the fire, their dance synchronized so well, they're one large chain of masculine dancing feet pounding the floor, stomping on it hard. It's all quite...masculine and sexy. They shout as they sing, and Nar takes Michelle's hand and starts pulling her into a circle in the front. She grabs my hand too. "Come on." Her fingers slip out as Mas growls loudly this time.

Fine. He's making a scene. "What is wrong you tonight?" I ask.

Mas touches my neck, gently drawing circles over my pulse. It reminds me of what Hart did to him. I don't know what this means for them, but for me, it's an oddly possessive gesture. "I brought you here so you can dance."

"I won't disappoint."

"I know."

I frown. "What's bothering you?"

"I'd rather you didn't dance."

I lift my chin. "There was this man I knew who was all roses and fuckshine. Then he started controlling me, telling me what to do, what not to do, and suffocating me and my career. I'm too old to repeat the mistakes I've already made in the past. I am dancing. Deal with it, Mas."

I spin on my toes, but Mas tightens his hold on my neck and spins me back. He kisses me, tongue and all, in that way of his that makes me feel like he's eating my face. Once done, he puts me at arm's length and lets go. There's sadness in his eyes. He's being so weird!

I walk onto the dance floor and join the males in their circle. Soon, I find out their stomping hurts my feet, and I'm not very good at slamming my heels against the hard floor anyway. Rising on my toes, I copy their steps, albeit in a way that suits me best. From the corner of my eye, I spot Hart joining Mas with another female, a human woman with white eyes and a round rosy face framed in curly light brown hair. She waves, and I wave back while Hart whispers something in Mas's ear.

CHAPTER NINETEEN

"**E**me will be leaving in the morning, I presume," Hart says over the music.

It only takes her a few rounds around the fire to pick up the steps of our traditional dance. At first, she follows, but then moves with the males in the way that only Eme can. She dances on the balls of her feet, sometimes even on her toes, her body light, floating over the floor. She's mesmerizing, and I notice Aoa has stepped back to watch as well. The males start clearing the floor, and soon Eme has the entire hall all to herself.

"Let's see how you feel about the games after her dance," I tell Hart.

"After tonight, I know everyone will enter. Eme is... graceful and pleasant. And also dangerous."

I glance at him. "If you know they'll want to compete, then you have to hold the games."

"No."

"Hart, for Herea's sake, the games are the way of the Ka tribe."

"True. But I have my own limits, and I prohibit the blood games."

"Hold regular games, then."

He chuckles. "Eme won't be appeased. She'll find a way to get her blood elsewhere."

"Let's sacrifice some Ra for her."

Hart shakes his head. "Ark will find out. Picking off Ra for sacrifices is a sure way to start another war. Besides, we have one repair system and a thousand-plus males I need healthy and fit. No games."

"Hart, I beg of you, don't ask me to return her."

Hart smiles. "Why not, Mas?"

"Because she's lovely, and you don't know her the way I do."

Hart parts his verto and shows me deep cuts on his thigh. "These cuts aren't healing. Imagine if males go after each other out there in the games. How many will return wounded?"

"They'll be away from her, so they'll heal fine."

"You don't know that."

"Neither do you." I clear my throat. "My wounds are healing."

Hart shakes his head. "Amti is with young. She will bleed when she delivers the pups. What do I do then?"

"Eme wouldn't hurt the young."

"Eme is a womankind with no idea of the divinity she's dealing with. But I do, and she has to be returned."

"Give her a chance."

Hart takes me by my shoulders and levels me with a stare. "Mas, you thick-headed bastard, I *am* giving her a chance."

"By ordering me to return her."

"Yes."

"A few more spans. I need a few more spans. You will see what I see, and she will favor us all."

"There's only one way Eme will favor us all."

"Give her the games. As many games as she wants."

"No."

"Hart, you're making a mistake."

"I won't change my mind."

I glance at Amti, and she nods, looking apologetic. Fuck.

The song finishes, and Aoa and Amti both clap. Eme joins us.

"I've never had a chance to watch ballet live before. Beautiful. I'm so excited you're here," Amti says, taking a flower from her hair. She tucks it behind Eme's ear.

"Her stay is temporary," I mumble.

Eme smiles, but I've seen her smile, and this one isn't genuine. There's sadness in her eyes, and it fucking bothers me. If she understands the Kai wants her gone, she doesn't show it.

"Ready to go home?" I ask Eme.

"Sure."

Aoa and Nar join us at the same time as the music starts again. Aoa claps. "Again," she says and grabs both goddesses to go with her. The moment they step near the fire, the smoke drops to the floor in an unnatural way. It swirls around their dancing feet, making us all move back. Hart scratches his belly. I scratch my arms. Males grumble all around us, and the ones playing change the tune to something old, so very old, eerie, and beautiful as the prayer smoke spreads around the hall, making us all inhale the bodies of goddesses.

I inhale a lungful, and instead of feeling light-headed, I have clarity of thought. I know what I have to do.

* * *

It's the middle of the night when Eme and I walk through the empty streets of Kalia, having left the party early. My tribe-mates will stay until dawn, or even past dawn. Only the males on duty weren't there. We haven't had a celebration like this since the night we retook Kalia from the Ra invaders. Back then, females didn't dance, so it wasn't quite as nice as this one. All males like looking at womankind. They're pretty, cute, submissive, and necessary for our happiness.

"You're quiet," Eme says. "Still having a crappy night?"

I throw a hand over her shoulder. "Did you have a good time?"

"I did. Everyone is very nice. Even the Wall."

"The Wall?"

"Your Kai."

I chuckle. The Wall. She's right about calling Hart that. I certainly hit the wall with him on Eme. He won't budge. It's not the first time we disagreed, but it'll be the first time I won't follow orders.

We make it back to my single-male room, and as Eme undresses, I shake my head, displeased I never thought about repairing some of the huts in Kalia. Had I planned with a female in mind, I might have. But it hadn't occurred to me that I'd have one, or even meet one, and I definitely won't compete for one, least of all Eme. I think I've earned her. I've bled for her more than once. And I'm gonna do the forbidden for her.

Nude, Eme gets under the pelts, wide blue eyes watching me. I push away from the door where I've been standing and watching her undress and get in bed with her. I bring her closer to my body, then tuck her under me. Moving a stray lock away from her face, I kiss the tip of her cold nose, never letting go of her gaze. I want to peer inside her soul, reach in there and touch the divine.

Eme spreads her legs, and I nestle between her thighs, kissing her gently, tasting her sweet mouth, swallowing tiny moans as she enjoys my fitness. She runs her hands up and down my arms, feeling my muscles flex as I kiss her neck and breasts and belly, lower yet. I swipe my tongue between her legs and lick her thoroughly until she gushes the juices I want to swallow.

I enter her with a groan. My eyes almost roll to the back of my head, and Eme arches her back.

I kiss her neck, lingering at her pulse, my gums throbbing. "In the tribes," I say, "we hold games and compete for a female."

Eme's listening while I move inside her. Her little hitches of breath and moans make it difficult for me to rein in the urge to flip her over and mount her and bury myself balls-deep inside her, pumping her full of my seed.

"Hart won't hold the games for you."

"Because I am Eme?"

I nod and kiss her and fuck her slowly, enjoying this moment because there's only one in a lifetime.

"I guess that's good in a way. Saves me the heartbreak when you refuse to compete."

I pause and blink. "How did you know I wouldn't compete?"

"I overheard. Put two and two together to make four. I'll be leaving in the morning."

I move inside her. "That's the thing, Eme. You're going nowhere."

She threads her fingers through my hair. "I've decided I am. I'll take my pod that's attached to this tower and leave."

"Mmhm," I kiss her and lift her leg so I can get inside her deeper. Her pussy tightens around my cock and flutters in tiny waves of pleasures as I fuck it. This time, my eyes do roll back. "You feel good, Eme. I could spend a lifetime in your pussy."

She smiles and throws her head back, exposing her neck. I run my tongue over her jugular. Eme trusts me. Eme trusts my hunter.

I pick up the pace.

"Sometimes," I tell her just before I suck a nipple into my mouth, "a male claims a female for his own. And there are no games. Such a male is shunned from the tribe because a female can breed only with him." I fuck her faster. "Eme, look at me." She blinks those pretty eyes, and I see the vast sea in them. I want it all to myself. Selfish prick.

I fuck her faster and snarl, angry at myself, but unwilling to stop.

"You're mine, Eme, and I'm not letting you go."

Eme's head bounces on the bed, and I pound into her faster, harder, lifting up on my arms. She grabs my biceps, digs in her blunt fingernails, trying to pierce my skin. From the bottom, she lifts her hips and meets my thrusts. The hip lift changes the position of my cock inside her, and Eme's pussy squeezes it hard.

I thrust once and arch my back, then shout as my hook disengages. My balls pump jets of seed inside her womb, making my cock spray every drop inside her. Grunting, I hang my head, breathing out the air that's been accumulating in my lungs. I feel lighter somehow, and the guilt of hooking her isn't even there, which makes me feel even more guilty.

I gaze upon her again. White eyes greet me, and my hairs all stand on end as Eme stares into my hunter soul. She opens her mouth and speaks in her old dialect, making me want to scratch everywhere.

"This womankind is gentle," she says. "I am her, and she is me. You will serve her, predator or else…"

Eme closes her eyes.

I cup her chin and give her head a shake. "Eme."

When she won't wake, I take my damn cock out and hover over her, worried sick. "Eme?"

"Hm?"

"Are you okay?"

"Perfect."

"Really?"

"Tired. Good night."

I clamp my mouth shut. I just marked a goddess. It's an epic moment in my life, and my goddess wants to sleep. But I have a feeling if I don't say what I need to say now, I'll never get a chance. "Eme?"

"Hm?"

"Is this what you wanted from me?"

A corner of her mouth lifts. "I favor you over the others. Many, many, many others."

I rest on my side and bring her closer. I don't know why I can't stop yapping. "You don't have to mention the others right now."

She smiles. "Your jealousy pleases me." Eme opens her eyes, then closes them again and rubs them. "I fell asleep." Her still-white eyes widen as if awaking from a dream. "I'm sorry. I'm exhausted, and the actual bed is great. I feel terrible, though." She covers her mouth the way Amti did after eating Sor.

I kiss her perky nose. "Good night." I should feel terrible guilt for marking a fierce goddess, Eme, who belongs to no one male. A pack goddess, no less. But I don't, and if I had to do it over again, I'd have hooked her that first night in the tent. Now, it's up to Hart. Eme and I can both stay, or we can both leave. No Eme. No Mas. A divided Ka tribe.

CHAPTER TWENTY

MAS

Anticipating my meet with the Kai, I couldn't sleep. I've been watching Eme. I'm always watching Eme. She's my favorite pastime, active time, any time, all the time. She's become my everything. While she slept, my mind played out at least ten scenarios. What's the worst that could happen? What's the best that could happen?

There's nothing worse than separating from Eme. I'm never separating from her. Maybe I've always leaned that way, just refused to admit it to myself. Becoming a hooker and admitting I want a female for myself means I limit my tribemates and their chance at enjoying female attention. I will answer for that.

It doesn't mean I regret it.

Despite my better judgment, before I even knew who she was or if she was alive, I returned to the Blood Dunes, one of the most haunted places on the planet. Something greater than myself pulled me toward the sands, and I couldn't let go. Goddesses work in ways we'll never understand.

It's past midspan, and Eme is still sleeping. Deep sleeping, with heavy breathing as if her soul rests. And maybe that's exactly what she's doing. I don't know what it must feel like for a womankind to carry the spirit of Eme inside her, but I think it would be exhausting.

Quietly, I get out of bed and dress, then leave for the Hall of the Fallen, taking in Kalia. Her streets are more deserted than before, but she's no less alive. Air traffic buzzes above, the river runs, the current splashing the rocks. Males stroke their weapons, chatting quietly on my left, and I note they're making bowls, painting them with brushes. Stopping, I hover over my brother Tis to read his scribbling on the bowl. *There must be games.*

"Lyu said that, no?" I ask.

Tis nods. "No games for us. Lyu will favor the Ra now, I'm afraid."

"So why are you praying to her, then?"

"She's Eme's sister."

"And?"

He lifts his gaze. "Wherever Eme goes, Lyu follows not too far behind."

"True."

"If we pray to her, she might come, and then maybe, finally, we'll have proper games. With Hart and Nar out of the way, I'm looking good for the win."

His friends boo him. Tis laughs.

I pat his head. "I'm off to meet with Hart. Seen him?"

Hise answers. "Pacing the hall."

Hart has two modes, brooding and pacing. "The usual, then." I turn to leave, but pause. "Why is he pacing?"

Hise smiles. "You think I asked? Nobody's been in there since last night."

"Did something happen last night?"

"He announced Eme is going back to the Blood Dunes and there will be no games."

"And how do you feel about that?" Nar's onto something with the feelings.

Hise purses his lips, thinking. " Feel… How do I feel? I am relieved. Nobody in their right mind would play for Eme."

"That's because you all do not have a mind."

Tis rolls his eyes. "Keep walking, fucker."

"Hooker," I correct him.

Tis stands. "Tell me you didn't mark Eme."

"I did. She is mine."

Tis slaps me.

I chuckle. "I really marked her."

"Why, hooker, why?"

"Eme stays in the tribe, or we leave the tribe together." Silence falls, and the males stare at me as if they hadn't heard me correctly. "I'm off to see Hart."

Bowls, knives, and brushes drop, and the males follow behind me. In the tribe, gossip spreads faster than Mae's fire, and by the time I make it to the hall for my confrontation with Hart, there's at least a hundred males crossing the bridge with me. As I approach the doors, I stir my hunter so my Kai can scent my aggression.

He's sitting on the throne, not pacing. One foot over the armrest swinging back and forth, he's cleaning his claws with a dagger. Nar's sprawled over the steps. He looks up as I march inside.

"There you are," Nar says.

"You're expecting me?"

"Shouldn't we be?"

I narrow my eyes. "No, not really. I don't descend to the hall often."

"But you have something to tell me this blessed span, don't you?" Hart asks, still cleaning his claws.

"I marked Eme. If she goes, I go."

Hart smirks. "Okay," he says.

"What?"

"I said okay. Carry on."

That's it? After all the turns and blood we shed together, that's all my Kai has to say to me. Carry on? I head for the door, and the stunned males part for me. Tis walks with me, and I stop him. "You're staying," I say.

"So you hooked? You're still my brother."

"This is your tribe. You're staying."

"We'll make a new tribe called Timas." He chuckles, trying to lighten up the collective sorrow. We, the Ka, have never split up. The fact we run and die as one is what has kept us alive since the beginning of our time. I claimed Eme at a great cost to these males.

Or perhaps they don't need me anymore now that we have peace. Still, I glance at Nar, who's smirking. Why is he smirking? I snarl and march up to him. I feel like punching someone. Might as well be my best friend. Nar stands and meets me halfway. Our chests collide.

"What's funny?" I growl.

"You're funny."

I pull back my fist and swing.

Hart's there and traps my fist. The fucker is fast. I push against his hold, and he pushes back, and we struggle, and I'm tempted to make him bleed. He points a dagger at his chest and cuts. Stepping back, we watch the cut close. Not a drop of blood leaks out of his body. He licks the knife. "Amti is having a barbecue tonight. Bring Eme." Hart turns and descends into his chambers leaving me...stupefied.

I look to Nar for answers. "What was that about?"

"I told Hart if he held the games for Eme, you'd kill the winner and give her the sacrifice she wants."

"I wouldn't."

Nar snorts. "You'd let a male take the prize?"

He's right. I don't admit it. It matters not whether I admit it, my tribemates know I get irritated when they touch the portals. I am possessive of my things and can't have people touching them. Portals first. Now Eme.

"The Sha-male said it's possible Eme ran her own games. Whoever she favors won. You bled for her on the Blood Dunes and lived. It's a clear win. Nobody can compete with that. Besides, if Eme favors one of us, the Sha said she will favor all. Therefore, Hart refused the games and forced your hand, hoping that when Eme was claimed by whomever she chose, the blood sacrificing would stop."

"So you two have been stringing me along?"

Nar smirks. "Amti said her people have a saying. Love is blind. She said when people follow the heart, they don't always see what's really happening." Nar fists his hand and puts it over his chest. "Feelings. Do you understand them?"

"I have chest pains," I admit.

He nods. "Yeah, me too. Weird as fuck. Those are feelings." He pats my shoulder. "You played best. Congratulations."

"I hadn't thought of it as playing."

"Three spans, two nights, and we have a winner."

I recall that first night and her saying *you win*. Then once more. How could I not have seen this? I've bled for her on more than one occasion, showed her I was willing to sacrifice my life for her, and now I marked her. What if the Om and Ra tribes had it right all along? What if our scriptures are biased toward Herea? They were written by the Sha, who are males, after all. I'll think on that another span.

I move to sit on the steps.

Nar sits next to me.

In the hall, the males take out their daggers and cut their palms, then cheer when they see the wounds closing up again.

"Imagine this beautiful thing that just played out in my

head," Nar says. "The Ra are invading. We're outnumbered, and they're already on the streets of Kalia, in the hall here, and suddenly, their wounds can't close 'cause Eme marked Kalia as her territory, and Eme won't surrender."

I visualize Ra bleeding in the hall, the bridge, the streets. Sighing, I say, "Wonderful imagery, but Eme is a womankind, gentle and kind, not a weapon of war."

"Eme will do what she wants. And you'd better honor that."

"Yeah. You know what I'm thinking, though? I gotta get back to my controls and do something about that one portal in the tent."

"Hm?"

I side-eye him. "I tried to erect a portal and screwed it up."

"That's a first."

I make mistakes. Everyone does. Not Eme, though. Eme is perfect. Rising, I pat Nar on the head. "You coming to Amti's barbecue?"

"That depends on what's on the menu," he says.

"Sor's leg."

We snicker, but it's not really funny, because when we get to the barbecue, Hart'll need to confirm a predator isn't on the menu. Nar and I part ways for the span, and I return to my room. I lean against the closed door and watch Eme sleep while I think about my new life. I marked a goddess. It's still surreal, but, like Nar and Hart, I'll get accustomed to the tingling in my spine, the hairs rising as I feel her divine presence.

Eme rolls onto her back and opens her eyes and turns her head. The white eyes greet me, lifting at the corners at first, but then widening, and Eme sits up, alarmed, looking around everywhere at once. "What's all this?"

"It's me and you and our chest pains," I say. "Don't be afraid. They're just feelings."

"Mas, there's a million things all over the room. Everywhere." She scoots back, looking to me for an explanation. Frowning, I remember. "Womankind can't see the portals until they're marked," I say, more to myself than her, because my next thought…

Eme interrupts, "Well, then, good thing I am."

I smile. "You slay me, Eme. With you, nothing is dramatic and terrible. You find…a good thing about everything. Why me, when you could've had anyone, packs of predators if you wanted?"

Eme sighs and worries her bottom lip between blunt teeth. "I'm still me even with this Eme girl inside."

"I know."

"Tatyana. Me"—she points to her chest—"thinks you're her hero."

I push back from the door and kneel before her, then scoop her up and bring her closer to kiss her belly, where my hook is firmly attached to her womb. "I will not be a servant to you, but I promise to be your hero till the end of our time."

I don't admit Hart was right. For Eme, I would've killed whoever won. I would serve her.

CHAPTER TWENTY-ONE

TATYANA

The thing that happened between Mas and me last night feels much like the morning after when neither lover knows what's next. Or maybe it's just me, the one who doesn't quite know what to do next, because Mas keeps kissing my belly, murmuring things about babies, and I lean back, thinking on said babies.

I've always wanted a child. I kept putting off pregnancy for work's sake, knowing I'd have to stop performing. As the years after Jason's arrest and my deliberate absence from sex and men went on, my chances of both retiring and having a baby seemed like a farfetched dream I'd never realize. Some nights, while cooling my feet, I'd think about how I'd dance till I was broken, maybe even booed off stage. For as long as I can remember, ballet has been all I ever did well.

The experience here has shown me I can fall in love again with a man who lied to me when we first met, who kept secrets from me. It's the same male who risked his life for me, defied the rules of his people for me, and went against his tribe's leader to mark me as his own.

"You marked me so my stay isn't as temporary as the Wall wanted."

Mas lifts his head from between my legs, where he was about to do what he does best. Eat me. He sits on the bed. "I did mark you to ensure you're protected. But that's not all of it."

"Do you think maybe you love me?"

Mas levels me with a look. "I don't think about it." He points to his chest. "I have swellings and pains and flutters in my chest."

"You're right about that." I smile. "I've always wondered where my forever will be, you know. I've pictured myself retiring somewhere on Mars or maybe Joylius with a man half my age who fucks me rough and serves me margaritas during the day."

Mas rolls his shoulders as if bracing for something. "Is the marking not what you wanted from me?"

I cup his cheeks. "It's better. What we have is better. I've finally retired. I'm going to have a baby at forty-something. I'm going to start living. A new beginning doesn't sound so bad when it's the start of something better."

"And you own a piece of land called the Blood Dunes."

I chuckle. "Beach property in tropical paradise. We should go back there sometime."

"We can go there now."

I nod. "Damn, those portals are fantastic."

"Eme, listen, we won't always live in this small room. I'll find a hut in Kalia soon."

"With a bathroom?" I ask.

"Yeah."

"Or not, Mas, since we have a beach property with a tent already set up only a few steps away."

"Do you want to go back to the Blood Dunes today?"

Hmmm. "I'm unsure why I feel strongly about that place.

I guess Eme really is around in me somewhere. Every time I tried leaving the Blood Dunes in my pod, there was always this gut feeling that said I should stay, that someone would come for me, that I would be rescued. With it was an internal knowing that I would stay where I am forever." At the time, I didn't want to believe it. I wanted to get back to Earth, even though I wouldn't have retired there anyway. The political climate isn't looking bright for the future.

"Eme reigned over the lands from the Blood Dunes. Her power lingers in the blood-soaked ground. It calls to you. Embrace the call. Accept that you are her and she is you."

"And you are mine, hunter," I say jokingly, though I kind of mean it in a very possessive way.

"I am yours."

CHAPTER TWENTY-TWO

MAS

E me's tanning on the sand. I climb up to her former campground to fix the broken portal I erected during the first night of Eme's games, and I recall how I even came here with a gift. In the games, we gift females things we think they'll like, and they pick the best one. I gave Eme a golden hairclip I made with my own two hands. Unlike my brother Tis, I suck at handmade stuff, so I spent spans making that thing. The events I shared with her are all clicking together and falling into place. Which only makes me more pissy that I didn't see it before Hart did.

Predator blood still fresh on the wet ground after a rain makes the campground appear as a damn battlefield. On the way to the tent, I stop and pick up a piece of my pelt and shake my head. I don't know why I thought anyone would compete for Eme when Eme demands proof of fitness delivered in flesh and blood.

I enter the tent. "Fuck!" I jump back out, then growl and walk back inside, sit on the log, and glare at Tash, the Ra tribal Alpha's older brother, who is lounging on our bedding. Technically, the Blood Dunes are a part of his earldom, and he caught me with a secret portal, not to mention hacking Feli's portal on the sand.

He lifts a pelt stained with my seed. "You fucked, I'd say."

"Tash," I greet him, trying to think of excuses. Nothing comes to mind.

He sits up and smirks. The beads in his black hair click against one another. He's shaved his face clean and painted his forehead black, and he's radiating aggression despite his calm demeanor. Tash, much like his younger brother, Ark, is a devious bastard and cannot be trusted. Sitting alone with him is ill-advised. If it were my Kai here, I'd never leave him alone with Ark's family, especially not in what is Tash's earldom, even if Eme walks the lands again.

"You are in my territory," he says. "What are you doing here?"

"Hacking Feli's portal controls."

Tash nods. "I heard." He points to the shimmering portal. "Where's this going?"

It's a portal hooked to a secret portal that takes me to the heart of your territory. "Vosna."

Tash's silver eyes flash. "That's Loma on the other side. Do you think I'm stupid?"

"Yes."

He smirks. "I never liked you, Blondie."

"I know. I'm smarter and better looking, with a bigger dick. My fitness rubs you the wrong way."

Tash's on me in a flash, and I stand so our chests can collide. He grabs my throat, and I grab his. We dig our claws into each other's flesh, and I try to choke him as he's choking me, then remember that if I bleed Tash near Eme, he might truly bleed out and die, and the Ra peace agreement with the Ka depends on his well-being. Ark needs Tash by his side, and if Ark's replaced, the Ra will attack again. We have three females and young coming, and now more than ever, we should preserve the peace.

I release him and lift my hands.

He keeps his grip on my throat. "I've killed stronger males than you, and some even in front of you. Don't disrespect me again."

I nod. He is right. He. Is. Right. Not only have I hacked their portal controls (again), I trespassed with no permission and retrieved a female who I then marked without games. In agreement, I nod.

Tash releases me, and I wipe the blood from the cut his claw made. The wound closes instantly. Tash is still bleeding, his gaze on my neck where my wound has closed. He wipes his blood, waits a few moments, then narrows his eyes. "You are poisoning your claws now to make us heal slower?"

Wow. What the fuck? "That's a very interesting accusation. Have you ever done that?"

"That's for pussies."

I smirk. The Ra are pussies. But I can't say things like that if I'm gonna have a nice chat with one of the deadliest pussies in the Ra tribe.

"So what are you doing here, Mas?"

"I brought my Eme for a swim. She's fond of this territory, if you recall."

Tash freezes like prey before the predator pounces on it. But he recovers quickly and wipes his wound again, then rubs the blood between his fingertips.

"The cut won't close," I tell him. "Eme favors the Ka."

Tash rubs his belly, scratches his arms. He's creeped out. Hart and Ark also get itchy when uncomfortable. Those two are so alike, much more than Hart would ever admit. Sometimes I think Ark is Hart's long-lost brother in the same way Nar is my long-lost brother. Because Hart and Ark are much the same, the wars this past decade were exceptionally brutal as the two males outstrategized each other. Hundreds of thousands of dead until they reached an agreement.

"Ark wants Feli's controls back," Tash says.

"I'll need the Blood Dunes portal for Eme."

"Have at it," Tash says and points. "This one you're gonna collapse now, along with the portal in Loma. And then I will give you the Blood Dunes sand portal. Consider it a gift for Eme the Bloodletter." He wipes his wound. Still bleeding.

"I agree."

Tash's wound closes instantly.

I itch my belly. There. Goddesses are so creepy! Clearing my throat because I don't think I'll ever get used to having a divine presence looking out for me, I exit the tent, Tash following behind me. Outside, we sit on the logs, both of us a bit freaked out with the pulse of power in the tent. I know he felt it too. He's itching again.

"Fuck, I hate this place," he says.

I chuckle. "I'm not fond of it either, but Eme likes it, so…"

"What kind of an idiot marks Eme?" Tash whisper-hisses. "I thought you were the smartest fucker in the lands?"

"Smart fuckers know a thing or two you don't." Here's a thing or maybe two nobody yet knows, and I'm thinking it. Unmarked womankind can't see portals. After marking, I think the hook releases a piece of our genetic material and makes the womankind more adaptable to our way of life. Namely, it ensures their survival among predators. In other words, the hook makes them fit and fit in.

Therefore, in order to guarantee successful breeding and the thriving of this alien species on our land, all womankind should be marked. But he doesn't know that, and neither does anyone else. My Kai and my best friend will find out tonight during our barbecue, where hopefully, Amti will serve us something Hart caught in the forest and not a sacrifice for Eme. Blessed be lovely Eme, of course.

Meanwhile, the Ra are gonna suffer until they figure it out, and maybe they never will, and oh, how my tribemates will enjoy watching them suffer. I smile.

"What?" he barks.

"You didn't wait here for me to collapse the portal."

"You killed three of my males."

"I did not. Eme bled them, as is her right." The one I cut with my ax maybe I did kill, but not the other two. "They attacked her." There were four so one lived.

"I don't care. She's with the Ka now, so you answer for it."

"You're not listening. They attacked."

"This is their land."

"Eme walks again!"

Tash smirks the way Ark often does when he's figured out how to take advantage of another predator. "I will forget it happened. We need access to the portal near Mount Omila."

"There's no such portal," I lie.

"I smell lies."

His case of vanity is worse than mine. "No, you don't."

I scrub the back of my neck. "Your brother promised my Kai females, and he hasn't delivered."

"Because we need the fucking warbird in Mount Omila."

"How many females are there?'

"Hundreds maybe. I don't fucking know. Didn't count."

Hundreds. Hundreds! "Your warbird in Omila isn't our problem. How you deliver the females isn't our problem either."

"Listen to me, hooker, Hart promised us access to the portals so we can move around and deliver. He gave us shitty limited-access crap we can erect on our own, and they're all restricted, by you, no doubt. So you want the females? I want the warbird. Besides, the Ra defend the planet. Land defense is a Ka problem."

"The Om you'll get in trouble with aren't land predators, and even if they were, they've never bothered us. We leave them alone, they leave us alone. You should've never parked there. The birds are gonna rise up against you. Ah!" I snap my fingers. "You're trying to save the Ra from Om invasions. Did Ark piss on their territory, hm?"

"Let me tell you what I think is happening there." Tash grips his knees and leans in. "The Om are picking off the humans. Sooner or later, one of them will figure out those are breeders, and once they do, they'll wonder where the delicious pretty prey is coming from. The moment they search for the bird…"

"They'll find it."

"Yes, genius. They're gonna take all the females."

"Ark promised more."

"Not without the warbird."

"How did you get out of there in the first place?"

"Emergency portal. Collapsed as we exited."

"Amateurs."

Tash stands. "Maybe, but you know and I know you need females."

"As do the Ra."

"As do we all. So what do you say for once in our lifetime, Ra and Ka work together? Ensure the females survive and thrive with us, not the Om."

I stand with him. "Amti's having a barbecue tonight. Come for dinner. If Hart's okay with it, I'll erect a dick out there for you." What? No. "A portal."

"What's on the menu?"

"Eme might wanna bleed you. Amti's gonna fry your ass. You scared?"

He walks up to me and smirks. "Only if they both suck on my erect dick. Want to watch?"

Motherfucker. I swing. Tash ducks, leaps from the clearing, and midleap breaks into a hunter. Show-off. I strip off my verto and let my hunter chase him. Jumping over the clearing, I land on a rock, Tash already almost at the sand where Eme, none the wiser, lounges on the beach. In the nude.

Snarling on my way down, I'm trying to alert her of another predator, but maybe she's napping, showing Tash her pretty and fit body. I want to kill him. Blood will spill. I'm racing down after him, thinking I'm gonna rip him to pieces when a portal pops up, and he jumps inside.

Screeching to a halt, I end up between two boulders, glancing between the space Tash vacated and Eme. She sits up, shielding her eyes from the sun. Standing, she starts stretching, and I recognize the same movement I've seen before. It's her routine.

The portals can wait. I'm going to watch Eme. She's so beautiful when she's unaware anyone is watching. She's even more beautiful now because now she is mine.

CHAPTER TWENTY-THREE

TASH

The peace between my tribe and the Ka affords me the privilege of attending my first barbecue in their Kai's private space, a secluded, guarded bath somewhere on Ka territory. "You sure have nice weather," I say as I wipe the soles of my boots on the fine Ka grass, leaving mud from the Ra terrain staining it. This will irritate the Ka and make me happy.

Next to me, Nar's eyeballing my foot, flipping his dagger between his agile fingers.

I spare him a bored glance. *Ka, please, I will dance with your dagger any span.* Snorting, I lean my elbows on my knees and pick up a stick to stoke the firepit.

Hart stands on my left, the scent of aggression rolling off him irritating my nose. I rub it, then sniff out the smoke from the fire, inhaling the body of whichever goddess their Sha-male has decided to celebrate today.

Amti, who can make me crazy, is sitting across from me with Aoa, who can fry me with a bolt of lightning much the same way that Amti fries cubed meat stacked on a wooden stick. They sizzle. She is *barbecuing*. A *barbecue*, Mas explained, is an event where friends get together and cook their already caught and prepped prey. Apparently, humans capable of hunting feed other humans who can't hunt, and the Ka have all gone crazy for eating cooked meat.

Except for Eme, who's munching on hers in raw form (as she should), a tiny smile on her lips whenever she glances at Mas. He returns the smile and winks, and I snort again.

Marking a goddess? It's a sin. The Ka collective has gone mad, and I need to get the business over with and leave before Amti gets bored and decides to make my head her new playground.

Even if it means no heir for my earldom and the end of my bloodline, I'm staying away from human females. I don't care if they're breeders or that Amti's scent, that of a pregnant female, makes my cock leak with need. Shocked at my body's response, I stare at my crotch.

Nar leans in. "You getting horny?"

"No."

He touches his nose. "We know the scent of arousal and hunger. Don't lie, Ra, or I'll make a pelt out of you."

"Nar," Aoa says and taps the log next to her.

He sits across from me, and the crazy Kas with their goddesses stare at me.

Hart's still standing, happy to brood and keep a watchful eye, as if I'd hurt his pregnant female, Ka or otherwise. I most certainly would not. We have honor, my brother and I, and we held on to it for dear life during our long wars.

"Mas?" Hart prompts his portal master.

Mas stands and flexes his fingers, then cracks his neck and walks behind me. Standing, I turn, sensing Hart has moved. He brushes his biceps over mine, no doubt a display of dominance.

"Easy there, predator," I say. "I come in peace."

Hart's jaw works. "Until you claim a female, you will not

understand. Keep your hands to yourself and your voice low and pleasant. Anything you say can and will be used against you."

A giggle sounds behind me, and I turn. Amti's smiling. "In the court of Ka," she adds.

I scratch my belly and watch Mas. I have no idea how Hart can stand being around her without scratching himself all over. Amti's presence is so very creepy.

Mas erects a portal, and I approach and peer inside the spatial opening, taking in an unfamiliar place on the other end. "Where does it lead?"

"Near Loma."

Loma is on our territory, and we hate Ka portals in our territory. "Care to explain?"

"Instead of collapsing the portal in the tent near the Blood Dunes, I used it and will care for it. The location is a secluded spot near Eme's Dunes, and many will stay away from it. It offers you the best chance of entry and exit from Mount Omila should anything go wrong."

"Who will control these portals?"

"You will."

I give him a blank stare.

"I have access. Naturally. Even if you try to block me, I'll override you. Don't waste your time."

Cocky little fucker. "How do I know you're not trapping me?"

"Because we need the females," Hart says.

Shocked at his blatant declaration of a vulnerability I could exploit, I turn up my nose and inhale more prayer smoke coming my way. Something blue flashes in the sky. Recognizing what it is, I whisper, "Hide the portal. The Om are scouting."

As the words leave my mouth, Hart busts into a hunter, Mas scoops up Eme, Nar takes the other two females, and the entire place clears out in a heartbeat. I blink, and there's no portal or anything amiss here.

Remaining calm while Hart's hunter is pacing, I sit back on the log and grab a large soft white cloth. I scrub the Ra markings off my forehead and drop the cloth over my ierto. Ka wear vertos, and the Ra iertos. The Om scout can't see what I'm wearing and may think I'm Ka, and it's best he thinks that. If he recognizes me as the Ra, he'll suspect we're up to no good. The secret portal near Loma leads to Mount Omila in the Om territory, where Ark and I hid our ship. Better not give the Om any clues we're up to no good.

Hart snarls and snaps his teeth.

I check the sky. A massive obsidian predator with red eyes and a matching red beak descends as fast as a shooting star. He's gunning straight for us. "I don't think this one is a scout." Herea's fine tits, he's big, the size of my fucking house.

Keeping calm, I wait for him to land when all I really want to do is join Hart in hunter and face off the Om. The pair of us could kill him. Hart's almost as strong as Ark, and my brother is the strongest hunter in the lands. Against the bird of prey, a single hunter doesn't stand a chance, but in pairs, we do.

The Om lands on the other side of the baths. His wings remain spread, no doubt to show us his size. I had no idea they grew this large. I think it's Omi, the equivalent of Hart in the Ka tribe. We don't have a Rai yet, but my brother will be it.

Seeing as Hart's furry, and Nar and Mas are likely preparing the Ka tribe for war, I lean my elbows on my knees and open my mouth to speak.

Hart roars right at my ear.

Ah, shit. The hooker blew out my left eardrum. I wipe the blood with the soft white cloth. "Gonna have to male up, Om," I say. "Let's see you."

Hart's all teeth and snarl, tail tucked, ears low, head almost touching the ground, back leg muscles tensing, preparing to leap at the Om. I pray to Herea that Hart can rein it in, and the feathery idiot gets on two feet and speaks.

The Om closes his wings and, in a flurry of feathers and bone crunching, stands on two feet at the other edge of the bath. Paws down, he's the largest male I've ever seen, with dark hair and an even darker beard. White and blue feathers decorate his braids. White feathers mean this is Omi, the leader of the Om tribe. Something's up, and I hope it's not my ship. Fuck. If the Om found it or suspect we landed there, it's sort of like pissing on their territory, and the birds hate intruders.

" Omi," I say and dip my head, keep my gaze on him.

He clears his throat. "Greetings, Ka."

"Greetings, Omi," I reply and glance at Hart, who's pacing. I bet it's Amti's pregnancy that's making him more aggressive than usual. It occurs to me I'll be speaking in Hart's stead, maybe even for both our tribes. Only a turn ago, Hart tried to chew off my ear. Blessed be peace between our tribes. Saved my ear, though not my eardrum.

"What are you doing here?" I ask the Omi.

"Visiting."

I chuckle. "An unusual and unannounced visit."

"Indeed. I am in need of a translator." He leans forward and sniffs, then draws down his eyebrows. "Why are you cooking your prey?"

The Ka pussies are making me look bad. "The... We are..." I throw up my arms. I have no explanation for the barbecue event.

"You land predators are weird," he says.

"Yes, we are."

"May I have the translator?"

"Sure. Yeah." I want him out of here. I reach into my

pocket and grab a unit, then flick it across the bath, aiming high over his head. The bastard snatches it effortlessly.

He smirks. "Thank you. I owe you a small favor. Small," he repeats. "Should you need to call in on the favor, tell them Nen sent you."

And with that, the Omi flies away as fast as he came.

I stand and get going. Before I leave, I say, "He has a female." That's who the translator is for. I'm certain of it.

Behind me, Hart says, "Then hurry up and deliver the females they haven't picked off."

I purse my lips and stop before the portal. "My brother would never ask. He's too proud."

"Not really," Hart says. "But go on."

"If he calls on you, would you come to his aid?"

"If Ark holds up our peace agreement, I would."

"I'll return with a ship full of females within two spans. I suggest you raise Kalia from the ruins." They haven't even started repairs on their huts.

"And whose fault is it that Kalia is in ruins?"

My stepfather's. "Fuck you, Ka." I step into the portal.

CHAPTER TWENTY-FOUR

MAS

Hart's pacing the hall. I'm standing guard beside the throne and tweaking the massive portal I've erected for the transition of over a hundred human females the Ra promised would walk through three nights ago. Nar's snarling and shouting, cursing the lying Ra, swearing on Herea he will hunt Tash and Ark from here to Ralia and back.

A portal of this size can transport an entire Ra army. We have no idea what's gonna come through it from Mount Omila, and we all pray the Om visit doesn't mean he knows the Ra breached the territory and the Ka tribe is gonna benefit from the Ra breach. The Om are fierce and feared predators. Nobody wants to war with them. Well, maybe Ark does. If that's the case, I wish the Ra the worst of fortunes.

Hart, despite my protests, has brought Eme into the hall with us. He said, in case of an invasion, she's our best chance of survival. I reminded him I'm perfectly capable of collapsing portals, and he's perfectly capable of fighting the Ra as he's done during countless incursions into Kalia, but Hart insisted.

My sweet Eme looks nervous. I know she's the Bloodletter, and I know she can drain thousands of predators with a flick of her wrist, but she's mine to protect.

At the controls where I would've run the games for her, I hover my fingers, anticipating whatever is going to walk through the special opening. Nothing so far, and we've waited in the hall on guard for two spans. Eme hasn't slept, and I might kill my Kai while he sleeps for exhausting her.

Energy tickles my fingertips. "Something's coming."

Hart strides up to the portal, but Nar beats him to it and peers inside, lingers, then looks my way.

"There's a herd of them," he says.

"Herd of what?" I ask.

"Womankind."

"Out of my way!" the Sha-male pushes past the Kai and Nar. I've never seen the old male walk faster. He peers inside and steps back, then growls, "Move away, Nar. Your ugly face will scare them. Let them see our sweet, pretty Eme first."

One by one, females of all shapes and sizes walk through the portal. I can hardly believe my eyes as the hall fills with them. They're tall, short, thin, plump, dark skinned, light skinned, and I've never seen so many females in my entire life. Something catches in my throat, and I swallow it as if it's a rock, then gather my wits and close the portal.

Eme grabs my hand and tugs. I sit on Hart's throne, and she folds into my lap. The females murmur among one another, forming groups like subtribes where they whisper in secrecy, gazes roaming all over the hall, stopping on every one of us and then Eme. They linger when they see her. Eme waves. "Welcome to the Ka tribe," she says. "Michelle should be here any moment to escort you to the baths. I'll meet you there. Don't be afraid. These aliens don't bite."

We do bite, but that's not important right now.

Hart's frozen, just standing there near where the wall,

likely in shock that we've secured over a hundred females. It will be the most glorious season of games my people have seen in history.

Eme sits on my lap, small cold toes resting on my thigh. She throws a hand over my shoulder and watches me. I sniff her hair, lick behind her ear, her scent and taste familiar and arousing, making my hunter want to purr in front of all these people.

Eme lowers her head, a blush spreading over her cheeks. She looks up and speaks in the ancient tongue that still makes my hair stand on end. "My dear aunt Bera sends her blessings. The Ka shall thrive."

I kiss her pretty lips and place my hand on her belly. My tribe shall prosper, and we three along with them.

***

Hi, hope you enjoyed Lured. One day I sat back and noticed I write New Adult romance so heroines 18-25 and I said let me do thirty and up and now forty and up heroine for a change. It was a pleasure to write a 40+ heroine and I think I might do one or two more in this series. There's something about a heroine same age as I that clicks with me. Maybe it's the sass. At 40+, I have less fucks to give than when I was twenty. I wonder if you feel the same way.

In any case, by now, you're mid-way through the Tribes and I wanna thank you for sticking with them. I love this world and building it as I go is one of favorite things to do. Let's see about that sky predator on the next page. I think you'll find him extra special.

CAPTURED TEASER

OMI - MEET THE BIRD!

I spy with my bird's eye something white, round, and unwelcome. It's wobbling back and forth as it floats on the river current that separates Om-ky from the Om-las tribal lands. The Om-las, land predators, are starting to emerge from their huts, creeping down the hill on their bellies.

I whistle to alert my people to the alien object and wait a few moments.

My brother and nest-neighbor a short flight distance away doesn't respond, so he's either not home or doing reconnaissance, convinced the Ka are trying to invade our territory again. Turns ago, during the Ka-Ra wars, he spotted one of the Ka pups skulking over our territory, and ever since, my brother has kept an eye on that part of the thick forest, waiting for the Ka to return so he can pick him off.

Where there's one Ka, there're many Ka, and none of them belong on Om lands. We pick off and kill intruders. Maybe ask questions later. Maybe not. This alien pod is intruding. The river current floats the wobbly round thing, and if the current carries it, the waterfall will shatter the pod.

The Om-las seem intrigued and cautious, still descending on their bellies, their red fur making it tough to pick them out in the sea of green grass covered with tall red wildflowers they've planted for camouflage.

The pod's now floating right under my nest, meaning it's a few thousand notches away, since I live on Mount Omila, the tallest mountain on Nomra Prime. Talons gripping the edge of my landing platform, I fluff up my wings and prepare for flight.

The Om-las are lining up along the riverbank.

The pod's door opens, and I balance with my wings spread as I lean over the edge, turning my head to the side to home in and sharpen my vision. Unfortunately, the door has opened toward the Om-las side, so they can view inside the pod. I observe the land predators' reaction.

On the other side of the river, the Om-las hunters clamp down their large ears and keep their tails tucked under their butts and their legs folded. Their teeth are bared, and they're drooling. They don't appear as if they're gonna attack. They're...tilting their heads as if confused.

I'm dying of curiosity now.

Is there live food in the pod?

A breeze ruffles my feathers, and I fluff them up. I'm not that hungry.

The pod's slowly turning my way, and I'm leaning over as far as I can, shaking my tail in anticipation of seeing what's inside. I spy legs. Chubby short legs in red shoes with a stick under the heel so the alien walks on props. It peeks his or her head out the door. Short, brown chin-length hair, perky nose, and only partly white eyes. Well-fed, I'd say. Would make a nice meal.

It's looking around, probably wondering where it crashed. The Om-las start creeping toward the alien, dipping into the river now, keeping their ears folded, their heads barely above the water as they swim.

Now, most alien species are food for us, and this one looks like a lost food item from space. I haven't had an alien in many turns, and I welcome a change in diet. With a sweep of wings, I take flight, heading for the alien.

The Om-las snap their heads up, their ears perking upright. I assume my targeting position. Wings folded, neck extended, eyes on the food, diving at top speed, wind in my favor. Inwardly, I chuckle. I'm gonna snatch it right out from under their paws.

One of the hunters lifts his head and eyes me with as much malice as he can muster. I bet it's the alpha of the land Om predators.

Ignoring him, I arrow toward the alien, who's none the wiser. Twenty-three predators on the land, one in the sky, and this prey is scooping up water and bringing it to its mouth to drink. Tsk, tsk, tsk. Too easy.

One Om-las circles around the pod, practically begging to be seen, but the alien keeps drinking, then retreats back inside the pod. The current picks up speed, surging the pod toward the waterfall. The alien is going go down with it. Based on what I've seen of the species' anatomy, it won't survive the fall, and since it doesn't have wings, it'll splatter on the rocks. No fun eating that.

The river dividing the land and sky Om is a fair hunting ground. Once the alien makes it to either side of the territory, we respect the boundaries. Eh, most of the time. If I want to eat, I need to move in.

I shriek, alerting the Om-las that I want the prey, and at the same time alerting the prey of the presence of a predator. I hope it'll run, and then I can chase it. The prey pokes its head out and gazes toward the sky. Brown eyes spot me, widen, and it screams at the top of its lungs.

The Om-las use their muzzles to push the pod onto their territory. I drop, as swift as Aoa's lightning. My talons wrap around the pod's opening, and I lift the object, noting it's rather heavy. Straining my wings, I swoop left and away from the river, the Om-las snarling behind me.

I cackle.

Suddenly, the load of the object feels lighter, and the Om-las start snorting, which in hunter means they're laughing. Under me, the alien's running. It jumped ship. Ha! Not boring after all.

I dump the pod and descend, ready to scoop up my food, when the alien ducks. I miss, twisting at the last moment before I would crash against the base of the mountain.

Rounding her, I land, inhale a lungful of air, and screech.

The prey, about one twentieth of my size, fists its tiny hands and screams back at me, then makes a run for a hole in the mountain. If it makes it inside, I'll have to shrink into male to yank it out of there, and that'll annoy me. In male, I'm slow, and who walks when they can fly? Not me.

I snap out my wing and cover the hole, then extend the other wing and crouch. The alien tries to run the other way, but I close my wings around it and bring it to my chest, holding it there while it punches me. I'm eyeing its struggle from above as I sit on the ground, and the Om-las keep snorting with laughter.

Eventually, the prey stops fighting and looks up. Big brown eyes stare at me. They're watery. My food is sad it lost the fight and knows it's gonna die. I contemplate playing with it some more, releasing it, letting it run around just to see how far it thinks it can get. I like playing with food. This one was too easy to hunt, though not boring.

I put the prey down.

It stays in place, even sits, wiping its eyes. It talks at me.

Breasts pressed together to make a vertical line draw my gaze. It is a female prey. With nice, juicy thighs. Mmm.

She keeps talking in a way that requires an agile tongue and strong throat muscles. Her voice keeps rising. Tears flow freely down her face, and she waves her hands about her. Pausing, she stares up at me.

I side-eye her.

She's quiet now, thinking. What's she gonna do, I wonder.

She takes off her propping shoe and throws it at my chest.

It bounces off and flies just past her cheek.

She's trying to kill me with her awkward shoe. I wish I had a translator so I could understand her. I'm sure I'd find it amusing. She doesn't seem to be begging.

Here comes the other shoe, aimed at my head. It hits my beak, bounces off, and falls next to my talon. I flick it and hit the alien in the shoulder.

She throws it back.

I flick it again.

Right at her forehead. Ouch.

She puts the shoe back on her foot and stands to get the other one, then puts that one back on too. The Om-las line their side of the riverbank, curiously tilting their heads. If I leave the prey here, they'll sneak across and consume her. I'm not that hungry, but she looks delicious. A fun and full meal to be sure.

I grab her between my talons, then take flight, her screaming making me happy. I bet she's a squeaker. I love squeakers. Gonna store the food inside my nest for later when I'm real hungry. Read more...

A SNIPPET FROM SENT BEAST MATE

MAYHEM

Having nothing else to do, I reclined back, kicked up my foot, and licked my teeth. Mmmm, not bad. Humans tasted differently depending on their diet and hygiene. The one in my mouth fed well. Maybe I should've kept him for supper.

"Reeeeagan," I called out again as I continued reading her file. "It says here you are…" I paused, unsure what to say about this one's profession. *Aerialist.* Wait a minute. It got better. *Hobbies: juggling.* None of those matched her former babysitting job, so I presumed she ended up babysitting when she couldn't find an aerialist job.

Or she didn't want to be auctioned and had scribbled nonsense on her paperwork. Nothing we hadn't dealt with before. A swift paddling and a nice warm meal tamed girls with attitude. She'd adjust within a week.

"I bet her pussy tastes like honey," Lore said. "Take a look."

Fine. I put her file aside and spared her a glance.

The girl had approached, all right. She stood on the first step with her mouth slightly open and her bottom lip trembling. She tucked it between her teeth. Her abundant, long, straight black hair curtained a face adorned with tiny freckles over her nose, and her shirt barely held together handfuls of tits. I concurred with my cousin. Cute. Would taste good if she were mine. But she wasn't.

"Eyes up," I said, because she stared at the floor.

The girl lifted her chin.

Gray eyes locked with mine.

Something cold ripped through my chest, and my lungs arrested. A growl escaped my chest. It felt like I'd died. I inhaled just to be sure I could. This response, the force of my instinct, meant only one thing. This girl was the spy. She was it, the girl I'd been waiting for. In an instant, auctions became a thing of the past, the whole room cleared out before my eyes, and all I saw was the prey before me.

I bared my teeth.

She peeked under her bangs, gray eyes wide.

My whole body roared to life, and even my dick hardened at the prospect of a cat-and-mouse chase. They'd sent her here to gather information for Men of Earth. Once they deemed her mission complete, she would try to poison her beast. Or kill him in his sleep. There was only one beast she'd deal with, and that beast was me. I rounded my chair, gave the crowd my back.

Lore stepped in front of me. "Stop with the crazy," he said. "It's making my skin crawl. Sit your ass down so I can buy her and take her downstairs. I'm gonna gorge on that one."

"She's the girl for me."

His eyes paled. A challenge. "I'll pay you."

"It's the girl we're after," I clarified.

Lore glanced back at the girl. "Are you sure?"

"Don't question me."

"What a shame. Proceed as planned?"

"Yes." I turned back and motioned her over. As she approached, the peculiar scent of my prey caught my nose. All the blood slid down to my erect dick. I wanted to consume her. It was a case of a hunter having its prey, nothing more. With my mating instinct muted in the background, my hunting instinct rode me harder than necessary because I really wanted New City for my future mate and me and for my people. This girl would give me all I wanted.

After I worked her and wrung her dry of information, I'd snap her in half and hunt the man hovering in the back of the room. For now, I let him think he got me.

When her front touched mine, I felt her tremors. With her head tipped back as far as it would go, she stared at my face. I bent a little and inhaled the scent of her sweet breath as her mouth opened slightly. My claws sprang out, and I fisted my hands so they wouldn't fly out and touch her. I didn't know if I'd rip her or hug her close and thank her for being here. Finally, I had a mouse to hunt. It would be a quiet hunt, but a hunt nonetheless. I didn't think I could get through another one of these auctions.

"There's blood on your face," she said.

"You'll clean it."

"Me?"

"You." I took a minute to compose myself, my face, as always, impassive. Then I twirled my finger, motioning for her to turn around. She narrowed her eyes as if she didn't understand the gesture. I sensed some defiance, but that was okay, because I'd train her. "Turn around," I clarified.

She wrinkled her nose and didn't turn, maybe because she didn't want to show her body. No room for shyness around here, so I spun her by her hips and ripped the shirt off her shoulders so her breasts would be bared to all. I didn't need to see her, because I didn't care what she looked like, but I knew the Men of Earth guy who brought her was here in the crowd, and I wanted him to see there was nothing different about this girl. Auction as usual. Women came; they stripped; we bid.

A growl escaped my chest, and the room silenced of whispers.

Lore's breath brushed my ear as he whispered, "Look a bit less excited if you can help it."

Certainly. I cleared my throat, and said, "Bids."

Silence.

As I stood behind her, my body against hers, we were skin on skin. My pretty prey felt so good, and I fell in love with the prospect of destroying her. Why not? She'd come here to destroy me. I swept my gaze over the quiet room. Why was nobody bidding? I snarled, "Bids!" I put a hand over her naked shoulder and felt her tremble under my palm. She should fear. Seconds passed. Nobody bid a dime on her. My tribe members didn't like her as much as Lore and I did.

Lore jabbed an elbow into my ribs.

"What?" I snarled again.

"Curb the excitement," he whispered. "Our males are confused. They think you want the girl, so nobody'll buy her."

I swept my gaze over my people again. On second thought, they all looked bewildered. What the fuck was wrong with them? Someone needed to buy her so it wouldn't look like I'd bought her.

"Oh man. Nobody?" the girl mumbled. I swiped a thumb over her pulse. It beat a mile a minute. I wasn't sure if she was pissed off nobody was bidding or if she was terrified someone would.

Did I even have any money? I patted my kilt, stuck a hand into my pocket, and got some of their green papers. "I got a twenty." I waved a bill. "The girl is a nanny. She will be my gift for Alpha Beast and his pair." Jamie had cut all ties with the Earthlings, and my people knew that.

They stood there like confused kids. "Certainly. This human is perfect," I said and found the middle-aged man in the back. He didn't come for the money. Instead, he tipped his gray hat and shrank back into the crowd. "I'll take excellent care of her." Read More...

MILANA'S BACKLIST

Dirty Wolf and Jake are exclusive to my newsletter subscribers
HERE!

Tribes:

Marked #1, Stolen #2, Lured #3, Captured #4

Read the complete Beast Mates Series:

#0 Virgin - FREEBIE, #1 Blind, #2 Wild,

#2.5 Goddess, FREE via my Mailing List,

#3 Sent, #3.5 Their, #4 Caught, #4.5 His, #5 Free.

Read the Complete Horde Series:

#1 Alpha Breeds, #2 Alpha Bonds, #3 Alpha Knots, #4 Alpha Collects

The Complete Hordesmen Series:

Hunger #1, Terror #2, Sidone #3, Fever #4, Dreikx #5, The Blind
Hordesman #6

Read the complete Dragon Brotherhood:

Rise #1, Burn #2, Storm #3, Fight, #4

Short stories in IADB World: Jake 1.5, Eddy #2.5

Read the complete Age of Angels series:

Court of Command, #1 • Court of Sunder, #2 • Court of Virtue, #3

ABOUT THE AUTHOR

Milana Jacks grew up with tales of water fairies that seduced men, vampires that seduced women, and Babaroga who'd come to take her away if she didn't eat her bean soup. She writes sci-fi fantasy romance with dominant monsters from her home on Earth she shares with Mate and their three little beasts.

• Sometimes she releases stories for the readers on her mailing list as they await for books in the series. If you want in, join other readers at http://www. milanajacks.com/newsletter/ •

Meet me at
www.milanajacks.com

Made in the USA
Columbia, SC
26 July 2021